"I'll Want A DNA Test."

"Of course," she said.

"I'll take care of it tomorrow."

"What?" She shook her head, looked at him and asked, "Don't you have to wait until we're back in San Pedro?"

"No, I'm not going to wait. I want this question settled as quickly as possible." He continued to eat, as though what they were discussing wasn't affecting him in the slightest. "We dock at Cabo in the morning. You and I will go ashore, find a lab and have them fax the findings to the lab in San Pedro."

"We will?" She hadn't planned on spending a lot of time with Nick, after all. She'd only come on board to tell him about the twins and frankly, she'd thought he wouldn't want anything more to do with her after that. Instead, he'd moved her into his suite and now was proposing that they spend even more time together.

"Until this is taken care of to my satisfaction," Nick told her softly, "I'm not letting you out of my sight. The two of us are going to be joined at the hip. So you might as well start getting used to it."

W9-ART-313

Dear Reader,

Is there anything sweeter than watching a strong man be completely befuddled by a baby? Just as there's something elemental about seeing a father meet his child for the first time. Something powerful and touching.

In *Baby Bonanza,* Nick Falco does just that. He finds out he's a father and meets his twin sons for the first time. Everything changes for him—and because it does, everything also changes for the mother of his babies, Jenna Baker.

I hope you enjoy reading their story as much as I enjoyed writing it!

Happy reading,

Maureen

MAUREEN CHILD

BABY BONANZA

Published by Silhouette Books
America's Publisher of Contemporary Romance

If you purchased this book without a cover you should be aware
that this book is stolen property. It was reported as "unsold and
destroyed" to the publisher, and neither the author nor the
publisher has received any payment for this "stripped book."

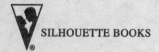

SILHOUETTE BOOKS

ISBN-13: 978-0-373-76893-6
ISBN-10:   0-373-76893-1

BABY BONANZA

Copyright © 2008 by Maureen Child

All rights reserved. Except for use in any review, the reproduction
or utilization of this work in whole or in part in any form by any
electronic, mechanical or other means, now known or hereafter
invented, including xerography, photocopying and recording, or in
any information storage or retrieval system, is forbidden without
the written permission of the editorial office, Silhouette Books,
233 Broadway, New York, NY 10279 U.S.A.

This is a work of fiction. Names, characters, places and incidents are
either the product of the author's imagination or are used fictitiously, and
any resemblance to actual persons, living or dead, business establishments,
events or locales is entirely coincidental.

This edition published by arrangement with Harlequin Books S.A.

® and TM are trademarks of Harlequin Books S.A., used under license.
Trademarks indicated with ® are registered in the United States Patent
and Trademark Office, the Canadian Trade Marks Office and in other
countries.

Visit Silhouette Books at www.eHarlequin.com

Printed in U.S.A.

MAUREEN CHILD

is a California native who loves to travel. Every chance they get, she and her husband are taking off on another research trip. The author of more than sixty books, Maureen loves a happy ending and still swears that she has the best job in the world. She lives in Southern California with her husband, two children and a golden retriever with delusions of grandeur.

To the ladies at Long Beach Care Center—
Christabel, Barbara and all of the others who give such
loving care to the patients—including my uncle—
who need it the most. You really are amazing.

One

"Ow!" Jenna Baker hopped on her right foot and clutched at the bruised toes on her left one. Shooting a furious glare at the bolted-down table in her so-tiny-that-claustrophobics-would-die cabin, she called down silent curses on the head of the man who was the reason for this cruise from hell.

Nick Falco.

His image rose up in her mind, and just for a second Jenna enjoyed the nearly instant wash of heat that whipped through her. But the heat was gone a moment later, to be replaced by a cold fury.

Better all around if she concentrated on *that* particular emotion. After all, unlike every other passenger aboard *Falcon's Pride,* she hadn't come aboard the floating orgy to party. She was here for a reason. A damn good one.

While her aching toes throbbed in concert with her heartbeat, Jenna cautiously stood on both feet and took the step and a half that brought her to a minuscule closet. She'd already hung up her clothes, and the few outfits she'd brought with her looked crowded in the narrow wardrobe. Snatching a pale yellow blouse off the attached-to-the-rod hanger, she carried it to the bathroom, just another step away.

It was the size of an airplane bathroom, only it also contained a shower stall designed to fit pygmies. In fact, the opening of the sliding door was so slender, Jenna had slapped one arm across her breasts when leaving the shower, half-afraid she'd scrape her nipples off.

"Really nice, Nick," she muttered, "when you upgraded this old boat and turned it into your flagship, you might have put a little extra thought into those people who *aren't* living in the owner's penthouse on the top deck."

But she told herself that was typical enough. She'd known what Nick was like even before she'd met him on that sultry summer night more than a year ago. He was a man devoted to seeing his cruise line become the premier one in the world. He did what he had to do when he had to do it. And he didn't make apologies for it.

She'd been working for him when she met him. An assistant cruise director on one of the other cruise ships in the Falcon line. She'd loved the job, loved the idea of travel and stupidly, had fallen in love with the boss. All because of a romantic moonlight encounter and Nick's undeniable charm.

Jenna had known darn well that the boss would never get involved with an employee. So when the sexy, gorgeous Nick Falco had stumbled across her on the Pavilion Deck and assumed she was a guest, she hadn't corrected him. She should have and she knew it, but what woman wouldn't have been swept away by a chiseled jaw, ice-blue eyes and thick black hair that just tempted a woman to tangle her fingers in it?

She sighed a little, set her hands on the sides of the soapdish-size sink and remembered how it had been from the first moment he'd touched her. *Magic.* Pure and simple. Her skin had sizzled, her blood had sung and her heart had beaten so frantically, it had been hard to breathe. He'd swept her into a dance, there in the starlight, with the Hawaiian breeze caressing them and the music from the deck below floating on the air like a sigh.

One dance became two, and the feel of his arms around her had seduced Jenna into a lie that had come back to haunt her not a week later. She fell into an affair. A blistering, over-the-top sexual affair that had rocked her soul even as it battered her heart.

And when, one week into that affair, Nick had discovered from someone else that she actually worked for him, he'd broken it off, refused to hear her out, and once they were back in port, he'd fired her.

The sting of that…dismissal felt as fresh as the day it had happened.

"Oh, God. What am I doing here?" She blew out a breath as her stomach began to twist and ripple with the nerves that had been shivering through her for months. If there were any other way to do this, she would have. After all, it wasn't as if she were looking forward to seeing Nick again.

Gritting her teeth, she lifted her chin, turned sharply and cracked her elbow into the doorjamb. Wincing, she stared into her reflection in the slim rectangular mirror and said, "You're here because it's the right thing. The *only* thing. Besides, it's not like he left you any choice."

She had to talk to the man and it wasn't exactly easy to get access to him. Since he lived aboard the flagship of his cruise line, she couldn't confront him on dry land. And the few times he was in port in San Pedro, California, he locked himself up in a penthouse apartment with tighter security than the White House. When she couldn't talk to him in person, she'd tried phone calls. And when they failed, she'd taken to e-mailing him. At least twice a week for the last six months, she'd sent him e-mails that he apparently deleted without opening. The man was being so impossible, Jenna'd finally been forced to make a reservation on *Falcon's Pride* and take a cruise she didn't want and couldn't afford.

She hadn't been on board a ship in more than a year and so even the slight rolling sensation of the big cruise liner made her knees a little rubbery. There was a time when she'd loved being on ship. When she'd enjoyed the adventure of a job that was never the same two days in a row. When she'd awakened every morning to a new view out her porthole.

"Of course," she admitted wryly, "that was when I *had* a porthole." Now she was so far belowdecks, in the cheapest cabin she'd been able to find, she had no window at all and it felt as though she'd been sealed up in the bowels of the ship. She was forced to keep a light on at all times, because otherwise, the dark was so complete, it was like being inside a vacuum. No sensory input at all.

Weird and strangely unsettling.

Maybe if she'd been able to get some sleep, she'd feel different. But she'd been jolted out of bed late the night before by the horrific clank and groan of the anchor chain being lifted. It had sounded as if the ship itself was being torn apart by giant hands, and once that image had planted itself in her brain, she hadn't been able to sleep again.

"All because of Nick," she told the woman in the glass and was gratified to see her nod in agreement. "Mr. Gazillionaire, too busy, too important to answer his e-mail." Did he even remember her? Did he look at her name on the e-mail address and wonder who the heck she was? She frowned into the mirror, then shook her head. "No. He didn't forget. He knows who I am. He's not reading the e-mails on purpose, just to make me crazy. He couldn't have forgotten that week."

Despite the way it had ended, that one week with Nick Falco had turned Jenna's life around and upside down. It was simply impossible that she was the only one affected that strongly.

"So instead, he's being Mr. Smooth and Charming," she said. "Probably romancing some other silly woman, who, like me, won't notice until it's too late that he's *nobody's* fantasy."

Oh, God.

That was a lie.

The truth was, she thought with an inner groan, he actually *was* any woman's fantasy. Tall, gorgeous, with thick, black hair, pale blue eyes and a smile that was both charming and wicked, Nick Falco was enough to make a woman's toes curl even *before* she knew what kind of lover he was.

Jenna let her forehead thunk against the mirror. "Maybe this wasn't such a great idea," she whispered as her insides fisted and other parts of her heated up just on the strength of memories alone.

She closed her eyes as vivid mental images churned through her mind—nights with Nick, dancing on the Pavilion Deck beneath an awning of stars. A late-night picnic, alone on the bow of the ship, with the night crowded close. Dining on his balcony, sipping champagne, spilling a few drops and Nick licking them from the valley between her breasts. Lying in his bed, wrapped in his arms, his whispers promising tantalizing delights.

What did it say about her that simply the memories of that man could still elicit a shiver of want in her, more than a year later? Jenna didn't think she really wanted an answer to that question. She hadn't boarded this ship for the sake of lust or for what had once been. Sex wasn't part of the equation this time and she was just going to have to find a way to deal with her past while fighting for her future. So, deliberately, she dismissed the tantalizing images from her mind in favor of her reality. Opening her eyes, she stared into the mirror and steeled herself for what was to come.

The past had brought her here, but she had no intention of stirring up old passions.

Her life was different now. She wasn't at loose ends, looking for adventure. She was a woman with a purpose, and Nick was going to listen to her whether he wanted to or not.

"Too busy to answer his e-mail, is he?" she muttered. "Thinks if he ignores me long enough I'll simply disappear? Well, then, he's got quite the surprise coming, doesn't he?"

She brushed her teeth, slapped some makeup on and ran a brush through her long, straight, light brown hair before braiding it into a single thick rope that lay against her back. Inching sideways out the bathroom door, she carefully made her way to the built-in dresser underneath a television bolted high on the wall. She grabbed a pair of white shorts, tugged them on and then tucked the ends of her yellow shirt into the waistband. She stepped into a pair of sandals, grabbed her purse and checked to make sure the sealed, small blue envelope was still inside. Then she took the two steps to her cabin door.

She opened her door, stepped into the stingy hallway and bumped into a room service waiter. "Sorry, sorry!"

"My fault," he insisted, hoisting the tray he carried high enough that Jenna could duck under it and slip past him. "These older hallways just weren't made for a lot of foot traffic." He glanced up and down the short hall, then back to Jenna. "Even with the ship's refit, there are sections that—" He stopped, as if remembering he was an employee of the Falcon Line and really shouldn't be dissing the ship.

"Guess not." Jenna smiled back at the guy. He looked about twenty and had the shine of excitement in his eyes. She was willing to bet this was his first cruise. "So, do you like working for Falcon Cruises?"

He lowered the tray to chest level, shrugged and said, "It's my first day, but so far, yeah. I really do. But…" He stopped, turned a look over his shoulder at the dimly lit hall as if making sure no one could overhear him.

Jenna could have reassured him. There were only five cabins down here in the belly of the ship and only hers and the one across the hall from her were occupied. "But?" she prompted.

"It's a little creepy down here, don't you think? I mean, you can hear the water battering against the hull and it's so…dark."

She'd been thinking the same thing only moments before and still she said, "Well, it's got to be better than crew quarters, right? I mean, I used to work on ships and we were always on the lowest deck."

"Not us," he said, "crew quarters are one deck up from here."

"Fabulous," Jenna muttered, thinking that even the people who *worked* for Nick Falco were getting more sleep on this cruise than she was.

The door opened and a fortyish woman in a robe poked her head out and smiled. "Oh, thank God," the older blonde said. "I heard voices out here and I was half-afraid the ship was haunted."

"No, ma'am." The waiter stiffened to attention as if just remembering what he'd come below for. He shot Jenna a hopeful look, clearly asking that she not rat him out for standing around having a conversation. "I've got breakfast for two here, as you requested."

"Great," the blonde said, opening the door wider. "Just…" She stopped. "I have no idea where you can put it. Find a place, okay?"

While the waiter disappeared into the cabin, the blonde stuck out one hand to Jenna. "Hi, I'm Mary Curran. My husband, Joe, and I are on vacation."

"Jenna Baker," she said, shaking the other woman's hand. "Maybe I'll see you abovedecks?"

"Won't see much of me down here, I can tell you," Mary admitted with a shudder as she tightened the sash on her blue terry-cloth robe. "Way too creepy, but—" she shrugged "—the important thing is, we're on a cruise. We only have to sleep here, after all, and I intend to get our money's worth out of this trip."

"Funny," Jenna said with a smile. "I was just telling myself the same thing."

She left Mary to her breakfast and headed for the elevator that would carry her up and out of the darkness. She clutched the envelope that she would have delivered to Nick and steeled herself for the day to come. The elevator lurched into motion and she tapped her foot as she rose from the bowels of the ship. What she needed now was some air, lots of coffee and a pastry or two. Then, later, after Nick had read her letter, she would be ready. Ready to face the beast. To beard the lion in his den. To look into Nick's pale blue eyes and demand that he do the right thing.

"Or," Jenna swore as the doors shushed open and she stepped into the sunlight and tipped her face up to the sky, "I will *so* make him pay."

"The sound system for the stage on the Calypso Deck has a hiccup or two, but the techs say they'll have it fixed before showtime."

"Good." Nick Falco sat back in his maroon leather chair and folded his hands atop his belly as he listened to his assistant, Teresa Hogan, rattle off her daily report. It was only late morning and together they'd already handled a half-dozen crises. "I don't want any major issues," he told her. "I know this is the shakedown cruise, but I don't want our passengers feeling like they're guinea pigs."

"They won't. The ship's looking good and you know it," Teresa said with a confident smile. "We've got a few minor glitches, but nothing we can't handle. If there were real trouble, we never would have left port last night."

"I know," he said, glancing over his shoulder at the white caps dancing across the surface of the ocean. "Just make sure we stay one step ahead of any of those glitches."

"Don't I always?"

"Yeah," he said with a nod of approval. "You do."

Teresa was in her late fifties, had short, dark hair, sharp green eyes and the organizational skills of a field general. She took crap from no one, Nick included, and had the loyalty and tenacity of a hungry pit bull. She'd been with him for eight years—ever since her husband had died and she'd come looking for a job that would give her adventure.

She'd gotten it. And she'd also become Nick's trusted right arm.

"The master chef on the Paradise Deck is complaining about the new Vikings," she was saying, flipping through the papers attached to her ever present clipboard.

Nick snorted. "Most expensive stoves on the planet and there's something wrong with them?"

She smirked a little. "According to Chef Michele," Teresa said, "ze stove is not hot enough."

Not a full day out at sea and already he was getting flak from temperamental artistes. "Tell him as long as ze heat is hot, he should do what I'm paying him to do."

"Already done."

One of Nick's eyebrows lifted. "Then why tell me at all?"

"You're the boss."

"Nice of you to remember that occasionally," he said, and sat forward, rolling his chair closer to the desk where a small mountain of personal correspondence waited for his attention.

Ignoring that jibe, Teresa checked her papers again and said, "The captain says the weather outlook is great and we're making all speed to Cabo. Should be there by ten in the morning tomorrow."

"That's good." Nick picked up the first envelope on the stack in front of him. Idly, he tapped the edge of it against his desk as Teresa talked. And while she ran down the list of problems, complaints and compliments, he let his gaze shift around his office. Here on the Splendor Deck, just one deck below the bridge, the views were tremendous. Which was why he'd wanted both his office and his luxurious owner's suite on this deck. He'd insisted on lots of glass. He liked the wide spread of the ocean all around him. Gave him a sense of freedom even while he was working.

There were comfortable chairs, low-slung tables and a fully stocked wet bar across the room. The few paintings hanging on the dark blue walls were bright splotches of color, and the gleaming wood floors shone in sunlight that was only partially dimmed by the tinted glass.

This was the ship's maiden voyage under the Falcon name. Nick had bought it from a competitor who was going out of business, and over the past six months had had it completely refitted and refurbished to be the queen of his own cruise line. *Falcon's Pride,* he'd called her, and so far she was living up to her name.

He'd gotten reports from his employees on the reaction from the passengers as they'd boarded the day before in the L.A. port of San Pedro. Though most of the guests on board were young and looking to party, even they had been impressed with the ship's luxurious decor and overall feel.

Nick had purchased his first ship ten years before, and had quickly built the Falcon Line into the primary party destination in the world. *Falcon's Pride* was going to take that reputation and enhance it. His passengers wanted fun. Excitement. A two-week-long party. And he was going to see that they got it.

He hired only the best chefs, the hottest bands and the greatest lounge acts. His employees were young and attractive—his mind shifted tracks around that thought and instantly, he was reminded of one former employee in particular. A woman he'd let get under his skin until the night he'd discovered her lies. He hadn't seen or spoken to her since, but he was a hell of a lot more careful these days about who he got involved with.

"Are you even listening to me?"

Nick cleared his thoughts instantly, half-irritated that he was still thinking about Jenna Baker more than a year since he'd last seen her. He glanced up at Teresa and gave her a smile that should have charmed her. "Guess not. Why don't we take care of the rest of this business after lunch."

"Sure," she said, and checked her wristwatch. "I've got an appointment on the Verandah Deck. One of the cruise directors has a problem with the karaoke machine."

"Fine. Handle it." He turned his attention to the stack of hand-delivered correspondence on his desk and just managed to stifle a sigh. Never failed. Every cruise, Nick was inundated with invitations from female passengers to join them for dinner or private parties or for drinks in the moonlight.

"Oh," Teresa said, handing over a pale blue envelope. "One of the stewards gave me this on my way in." She smiled as she handed it over. "Yet another lonely lady looking for companionship? Seems you're still the world's favorite love god."

Nick knew she was just giving him a hard time—like always—yet this time her words dug at him. Shifting uncomfortably in his chair, he thought about it, tried to figure out why. He was no monk, God knew. And over the years he'd accepted a lot of invitations from women who didn't expect anything more than a good time and impersonal sex.

But damned if he could bring himself to get interested in the latest flurry of one-night-stand invitations, either. The cards and letters had been sitting on his desk since early this morning and he hadn't bothered to open one yet. He knew what he'd find when he started going through them.

Panties. Cabin keys. Sexy photos designed to tempt.

And not a damned one of them would mean anything to him.

Hell, what did that say about him? Laughing silently at himself, Nick acknowledged that he really didn't want to know. Maybe he'd been spending too much time working lately. Maybe what he needed was just what these ladies were offering. He'd go through the batch of invites, pick out the most intriguing one and spend a few relaxing hours with a willing woman.

Just what the doctor ordered.

Teresa was still holding the envelope out to him and there was confusion in her eyes. He didn't want her asking any questions, so he took the envelope and idly slid his finger under the seal. Deliberately giving her a grin and a wink, he said, "You think it's easy being the dream of millions?"

Now Teresa snorted and, shaking her head, muttering something about delusional males, she left the office.

When she was gone, he sat back and thoughtfully looked at the letter in his hand. Pale blue envelope, tidy handwriting. Too small to hold a pair of lacy thong panties. Too narrow to be hiding away a photo. Just the right size for a cabin key card though.

"Well, then," he said softly, "let's see who you are. Hope you included a photo of yourself. I don't do blind dates."

Chuckling, Nick pulled the card from the envelope and glanced down at it. There was a photo all right. Laughter died instantly as he looked at the picture of two babies with black hair and pale blue eyes.

"What the hell?" Even while his brain started racing and his heartbeat stuttered in his chest, he read the scrawled message beneath the photo:

"Congratulations, Daddy. It's twins."

Two

She wasn't ready to give up the sun.

Jenna set her coffee cup down on the glass-topped table, turned her face to the sky and let the warm, late-morning sunshine pour over her like a blessing. Despite the fact that there were people around her, laughing, talking, diving into the pool, sending walls of water up in splashing waves, she felt alone in the light. And she really wasn't ready to sink back into the belly of the ship.

But she'd sent her note to Nick. And she'd told him where to find her. In that tiny, less-than-closet-size cabin. So she'd better be there when he arrived. With a sigh, she stood, slung her bag over her left shoulder and threaded her way through the crowds lounging on the Verandah Deck.

Someone touched her arm and Jenna stopped.

"Leaving already?" Mary Curran was smiling at her, and Jenna returned that smile with one of her own.

"Yeah. I have to get back down to my cabin. I um, have to meet someone there." At least, she was fairly certain Nick would show up. But what if he didn't? What if he didn't care about the fact that he was the father of her twin sons? What if he dismissed her note as easily as he'd deleted all of her attempts at e-mail communication?

A small, hard knot formed in the pit of her stomach. She'd like to see him try, that's all. They were on a ship in the middle of the ocean. How was he going to escape her? Nope. Come what may, she was going to have her say. She was going to face him down, at last, and tell him what she'd come to say.

"Oh God, honey." Mary grimaced and gave a dramatic shudder. "Do you really want to have a conversation down in the pit?"

Jenna laughed. "The pit?"

"That's what my husband, Joe, christened it in the middle of the night when he nearly broke his shin trying to get to the bathroom."

Grinning, Jenna said, "I guess the name fits all right. But yeah. I have to do it there. It's too private to be done up here."

Mary's eyes warmed as she looked at Jenna and said, "Well, then, go do whatever it is you have to do. Maybe I'll see you back in the sunshine later?"

Jenna nodded. She knew how cruise passengers tended to bond together. She'd seen it herself in the time she'd actually worked for Falcon Cruises. Friendships formed fast and furiously. People who were in relatively tight quarters—stuck on a ship in the middle of the ocean—tended to get to know each other more quickly than they might on dry land.

Shipboard romances happened, sure—just look what had happened to her. But more often, it was other kinds of relationships that bloomed and took hold. And right about now, Jenna decided, she could use a friendly face.

"You bet," she said, giving Mary a wide smile. "How about margaritas on the Calypso Deck? About five?"

Delighted, Mary beamed at her. "I'll be there."

As Jenna walked toward the elevator, she told herself that after her upcoming chat with Nick, she was probably going to *need* a margarita or two.

Nick jolted to his feet so fast, his desk chair shot backward, the wheels whirring against the wood floor until the chair slammed into the glass wall behind him.

"Is this a *joke?*"

Nick held the pale blue card in one tight fist and stared down at two tiny faces. The babies were identical except for their expressions. One looked into the camera and grinned, displaying a lot of gum and one deep dimple. The other was watching the picture taker with a serious, almost thoughtful look on his face.

And they both looked a hell of a lot like *him.*

"Twins?"

In an instant, emotions he could hardly name raced

through him. Anger, frustration, confusion and back to anger again. How the hell could he be a father? Nobody he knew had been pregnant. This couldn't be happening. He glanced up at the empty office as if half expecting someone to jump out, shout, "You've just been punk'd," and let him off the hook. But there were no cameras. There was no joke.

This was someone's idea of serious.

Well, hell, he told himself, it wasn't the first time some woman had tried to slap him with a paternity suit. But it was for damn sure the first time the gauntlet had been thrown down in such an imaginative way.

"Who, though?" He grabbed the envelope up, but only his name was scrawled across the front in a small, feminine hand. Turning over the card he still held, he saw more of that writing:

"We need to talk. Come to cabin 2A on the Riviera Deck."

"Riviera Deck." Though he hated like hell to admit it, he wasn't sure which deck that was. He had a lot of ships in his line and this was his first sail on this particular one. Though he meant to make *Falcon's Pride* his home, he hadn't had the chance yet to explore it from stem to stern as he did all the ships that carried his name.

For now, he stalked across the room to the framed set of detailed ship plans hanging on the far wall of his office. He'd had one done for each of the ships in his line. He liked looking at them, liked knowing that he was familiar with every inch of every ship. Liked knowing that he'd succeeded in creating the dream he'd started more than ten years before.

But at the moment, Nick wasn't thinking of his cruise line or of business at all. Now all he wanted to do was find the woman who'd sent him this card so he could assure himself that this was all some sort of mistake.

Narrowing his pale blue eyes, he ran one finger down the decks until he found the one he was looking for. Then he frowned. According to this, the Riviera Deck was *below* crew quarters.

"What the hell is going on?" Tucking the card with the pictures of the babies into the breast pocket of his white, short-sleeved shirt, he half turned toward the office door and bellowed, *"Teresa!"*

The door flew open a few seconds later and his assistant rushed in, eyes wide in stunned surprise. "Geez, what's wrong? Are we on fire or something?"

He ignored the attempt at humor, as well as the look of puzzlement on her face. Stabbing one finger against the glass-covered ship plans, he said only, "Look at this."

She hurried across the room, glanced at the plans, then shifted a look at him. "What exactly am I looking at?"

"This." He tapped his finger against the lowest deck on the diagram. "The Riviera Deck."

"Uh-huh."

"There are people staying down there."

"Oh."

Pleased that she'd caught on so fast, Nick said, "When the ship came out of refit ready for passengers,

I said specifically that those lower cabins weren't to be used."

"Yeah, you did, boss." She actually winced, whipped out her PDA and punched a few keys. "I'll do some checking. Find out what happened."

"You do that," he said, irritated as hell that someone, somewhere, hadn't paid attention to him. "For right now, though, find out how many of those cabins are occupied."

"Right."

While Teresa worked her electronic wizardry, Nick looked back at the framed plans and shook his head. Those lower cabins were too old, too small to be used on one of his ships. Sure, they'd undergone some refurbishing during the refit, but having them and using them were two different things. Those cabins, small and dark and cramped, weren't the kind of image Nick wanted associated with his cruise line.

"Boss?" Teresa looked at him. "According to the registry, only two of the five cabins are being used."

"That's something, anyway. Who's down there?"

"1A is occupied by a Joe and Mary Curran."

He didn't know any Currans and besides, the card had come from whoever was in the only other occupied cabin on that deck.

So he waited.

"2A is…" Teresa's voice trailed off and Nick watched as his usually unflappable assistant chewed at her bottom lip.

That couldn't be good.

"What is it?" When she didn't answer right away, he demanded, "Just tell me who's in the other cabin."

"Jenna," Teresa said and blew out a breath. "Jenna Baker's in 2A, Nick."

Nick made record time getting down to the Riviera Deck, and by the time he reached it, he'd already made the decision to close up this deck permanently. Damned if he'd house his paying guests in what amounted to little more than steerage.

Stepping off the elevator, he hit his head on a low cross beam and muttered a curse. The creaks and groans of the big ship as it pushed through the waves echoed through the narrow passageway like ghosts howling. The sound of the water against the hull was a crushing heartbeat and it was so damned dark in the abbreviated hallway, even the lights in the wall sconces barely made a dent in the blackness. And the hall itself was so narrow he practically had to traverse it sideways. True, it was good business to make sure you provided less expensive rooms, but he'd deal with that another way. He'd be damned if his passengers would leave a cruise blinking at the sun like bats.

With his head pounding, his temper straining on a tight leash, he stopped in front of 2A, took a breath and raised his right fist to knock. Before he could, the narrow door was wrenched open and there she stood.

Jenna Baker.

She shouldn't have still been able to affect him. He'd had her after all. Had her and then let her go more than a year ago. So why then was he suddenly struck by the turquoise-blue of her eyes? Why did that tight, firm mouth make him want to kiss her until her lips eased apart and let him back in? Why did the fact that she looked furious make his blood steam in his veins? What the hell did *she* have to be mad about?

"I heard you in the hall," she said.

"Good ears," he conceded. "Considering all the other noises down here."

A brief, tight smile curved her mouth. "Yeah, it's lovely living in the belly of the beast. When they raise anchor it's like a symphony."

He hadn't considered that, but he was willing to bet the noise was horrific. Just another reason to seal up these rooms and never use them again. However, that was for another time. What he wanted now were answers.

"Good one," he said. "That's why you're here, then? To talk about the ship?"

"You know why I'm here."

He lifted one hand to the doorjamb and leaned in toward her. "I know what you'd like me to think. The question is, why? Why now? What're you after, Jenna?"

"I'm not going to talk about this in the hall."

"Fine." He stepped inside, moving past her, but the quarters were so cramped, their chests brushed together and he could almost feel his skin sizzle.

It had been like that from the beginning. The moment he'd touched her that first night in the moonlight, he'd felt a slam of something that was damn near molten sliding through him. And it seemed that time hadn't eased it back any.

He got a grip on his hormones, took two steps until he was at the side of a bed built for a sixth-grader, then turned around to glare at her. God, the cabin was so small it felt as though the walls were closing in on him and, truth to tell, they wouldn't have far to move. He felt as if he should be slouching to avoid skimming the top of his head along the ceiling. Every light in the cabin was on and it still looked like twilight.

But Nick wasn't here for the ambience and there was nothing he could do about the rooms at the moment. Now all he wanted was an explanation. He waited for her to shut the door, sealing the two of them into the tiny cracker box of a room before he said, "What's the game this time, Jenna?"

"This isn't a game, Nick," she said, folding her arms over her chest. "It wasn't a game then, either."

"Right." He laughed and tried not to breathe deep. The scent of her was already inside him, the tiny room making him even more aware of it than he would have been ordinarily. "You didn't *want* to lie to me. You had no choice."

Her features tightened. "Do we really have to go over the old argument again?"

He thought about it for a moment, then shook his head. He didn't want to look at the past. Hell. He didn't want to be here *now*. "No, we don't. So why don't you just say what it is you have to say so we can be done."

"Always the charmer," she quipped.

He shifted from one foot to the other and banged his elbow on the wall. "Jenna…"

"Fine. You got my note?"

He reached into the pocket of his shirt, pulled out the card, glanced at the pictures of the babies, then handed it to her. "Yeah. I got it. Now how about you explain it?"

She looked down at those two tiny faces and he saw her lips curve slightly even as her eyes warmed. But that moment passed quickly as she lifted her gaze to him and skewered him with it. "I would have thought the word *daddy* was fairly self-explanatory."

"Explain, anyway."

"Fine." Jenna walked across the tiny room, bumped Nick out of her way with a nudge from her hip that had him hitting the wall and then bent down to drag a suitcase out from under her bed. The fact that she could actually *feel* his gaze on her butt while she did it only annoyed her.

She would not pay any attention to the rush of heat she felt just being close to him again. She would certainly not acknowledge the jump and stutter of her heartbeat, and if certain other of her body parts were warm and tingling, she wasn't going to admit to that, either.

Dragging the suitcase out, she went to lift it, but Nick was there first, pushing her fingers aside to hoist the bag onto the bed. If her skin was humming from that one idle touch, he didn't have to know it, did he?

She unzipped the bag, pulled out a blue leather scrapbook and handed it to him. "Here. Take a look. Then we'll talk more."

The book seemed tiny in his big, tanned hands. He

barely glanced at it before shooting a hard look at her again. "What's this about?"

"Look at it, Nick."

He did. The moment she'd been waiting so long for stretched out as the seconds ticked past. She held her breath and watched his face, the changing expressions written there as he flipped through the pages of pictures she'd scrapbooked specifically for this purpose. It was a chronicle of sorts. Of her life since losing her job, discovering she was pregnant and then the birth of the twins. In twenty hand-decorated pages, she'd brought him up to speed on the last year and a half of her life.

Up to speed on his sons. The children he'd created and had never met.

The only reason she was here, visiting a man who'd shattered her heart without a backward glance.

When he was finished, his gaze lifted to hers and she could have sworn she saw icicles in his eyes.

"I'm supposed to believe that I'm the father of your babies?"

"Take another look at them, Nick. They both look just like you."

He did, but his features remained twisted into a cynical expression even while his eyes flashed with banked emotion. "Lots of people have black hair and blue eyes."

"Not all of them have dimples in their left cheek." She reached out, flipped to a specific page and pointed. "Both of your sons do. Just like yours."

He ran one finger over the picture of the boys as if he could somehow touch them with the motion, and that small action touched something in Jenna. For one brief instant, Nick Falco looked almost…vulnerable.

It didn't last long, though. His mouth worked as if he were trying to bite back words fighting desperately to get out. Finally, as if coming to some inner decision, he nodded, blew out a breath and said, "For the sake of argument, let's say they are mine."

"They are."

"So why didn't you tell me before? Why the hell would you wait until they're, what…?"

"Four months old."

He looked at the pictures again, closed the book and held on to it in one tight fist. "Four months old and you didn't think I should know?"

So much for the tiny kernel of warmth she'd almost experienced.

"You're amazing. You ignore me for months and now you're upset that I didn't contact you?"

"What're you talking about?"

Jenna shook her head and silently thanked heaven that she'd been smart enough to not only keep a log of every e-mail she'd ever sent him, but had thought to print them all out and bring them along. Dipping back into the suitcase, she whipped a thick manila envelope out and laid it atop the scrapbook he was still holding. "There. E-mails. Every one I sent you. They're all dated. You can see that I sent one at least once a week. Sometimes twice. I've been trying to get hold of you for more than a year, Nick."

He opened the envelope as she talked, and flipped quickly through the printouts.

"I—" He frowned down at the stack of papers.

She took advantage of his momentary speechlessness. "I've been trying to reach you since I first found out I was pregnant, Nick."

"How was I supposed to know that *this* is what you were trying to tell me?"

"You might have read one or two of them," Jenna pointed out and managed to hide the hurt in her voice.

He scowled at her. "How the hell could I have guessed you were trying to tell me I was a father? I just thought you were after money."

She hissed in a breath as the insult of that slapped at her. Bubbling with fury, Jenna really had to fight the urge to give him a swift kick. How like Nick to assume that any woman who was with him was only in it for what she could get from him. But then, he'd spent most of the past ten years surrounding himself with the very users he'd suspected her of being. People who wanted to be seen with him because he was one of the world's most eligible billionaires. Those hangers-on wanted to be in his inner circle because that's where the excitement was and it made them feel important, to be a part of Nick's world.

All Jenna had wanted was his arms around her. His kiss. His whispers in the middle of the night. Naturally, he hadn't believed her.

Now things were different. He had responsibilities that she was here to see he stood up to. After all, she hadn't come here for herself. She'd come for her kids. For *his* sons.

"I wasn't interested in your money back then, Nick. But things have changed and now, I *am* after money," she said and saw sparks flare in his icy eyes. "It's called child support, Nick. And your sons deserve it."

He stared at her. "Child support."

"That's right." She lifted her chin even higher. "If I only had myself to think about, I wouldn't be here, believe me. So don't worry, I'm not here to take advantage of you. I'm not looking for a huge chunk of the Falco bank account."

"Is that right?"

"That's right. I started my own business and it's doing fine," she said, a hint of pride slipping into her tone while she spoke. "But twins make every expense doubled and I just can't do it all on my own." Lifting her gaze to meet his, she said, "When you never responded to my e-mails, I told myself you didn't deserve to know your babies. And if I weren't feeling a little desperate I wouldn't be here at all. Trust me, if you think I'm enjoying being here like this, you're crazy."

"So you would have hidden them from me?" His voice was low, soft and just a little dangerous.

Jenna wasn't worried. Nick might be an arrogant, self-satisfied jerk, but physically dangerous to her or any other woman, he wasn't. "If you mean would I hide the fact that their father couldn't care less about them from my sons…then, yes. That's just what I'll do."

"If they are my sons," he whispered, "no one will keep me from them."

A flicker of uneasiness sputtered in Jenna's chest, but she told herself not to react. Physical threats meant nothing, but the thought of him challenging her for custody of their children did. Even as she considered it, though, she let the worry dissipate. Babies weren't part of Nick's world, and no matter what he said at the moment, he would never give up the life he had for one that included double diaper duty.

"Nick, we both know you have no interest in being a father."

"You have no idea what I do or don't care about, Jenna." He moved in close, taking that one small step that brought his body flush to hers. Jenna hadn't been prepared for the move and sucked in a gulp of air as his chest pressed into hers.

She looked up into his eyes and felt her knees wobble a little at the intensity of his stare. He cupped her cheek in one hand, and the heat of his skin seeped into hers, causing a flush of warmth that slid through her like sweet syrup.

"I promise you, though," he murmured, dipping his head in as if he were going to kiss her and stopping just a breath away from her lips, "you will find out."

Three

She ducked her head and slapped his hand away and even *that* contact felt too damn good. Nick stepped back and away from her, which, in that cabin, meant that he was halfway out the door. So once he felt as though he could look at her without wanting to wrap his hands in her hair and pull her mouth to his, he shifted his gaze to hers.

"I don't have the time to go through this right now."

She smirked at him, folded her arms over her chest in a classic defensive posture. "Oh, sure, worlds to conquer, women to seduce. Busy, busy."

"Clever as ever, I see." He didn't even want to admit to himself how much he'd missed that smart mouth of hers. Always a retort. Always a dig, putting him in his place, deflating his ego before it had a chance to expand.

There weren't many people like Jenna in his life. Mostly, those he knew were too busy kissing his ass to argue with him. Everyone but Teresa, that is. And of course, Jenna. But she wasn't a part of his life anymore.

"We'll have dinner tonight. My suite."

"I don't think so."

"You came here to talk to me, right?"

"Yes, but—"

"So we'll talk. Seven o'clock."

Before she could argue, stall or whatever else might come into her too-quick mind, he opened the door and left her cabin. He took a breath in the dark hall, then headed for the elevator that would take him out of the bowels of the ship back into the light.

By five o'clock, she was more than ready to meet Mary for margaritas.

Jenna'd left her tiny, hideous, airless cabin only a few minutes after Nick had. Frankly, his presence had been practically imprinted on the minuscule space and had made the cabin seem even smaller than it actually was. And she hadn't thought that would have been possible.

But he'd shaken her more than she'd thought he would. Just being near him again had awakened feelings and emotions she'd trained herself more than a year ago to ignore. Now they were back and she wasn't sure how to handle them. After all, it wasn't as if she had a lot of experience with this sort of thing. Before Nick, there'd been only one other man in her life, and he hadn't come close to affecting her in the way Nick had. Of course, since Nick, the only men in her life preferred drooling on her shoulder to slow dances in the dark.

Just thinking about her boys brought an ache to Jenna's heart. She'd never left them before, and though she knew the twins were in good hands, she hated not being with them.

"But I'm on this boat for their sakes," she reminded herself sternly.

With that thought in mind, her gaze swept the interior of Captain Jack's Bar and Lounge. Like everywhere else on this ship, Nick hadn't skimped. The walls were pale wood that gleamed in the light glinting down on the crowd from overhead chandeliers shaped like ship's wheels. The bar was a slinky curve of pale wood with a granite top the color of molten honey.

Conversations flowed in a low rumble of sound that was punctuated by the occasional clink of crystal or a high-pitched laugh. First day at sea and already the party had begun.

Well, for everyone but Jenna. She hadn't exactly been in celebration mode after Nick left her cabin.

In fact, Jenna'd spent most of the day lying on a chaise on the Verandah Deck, trying to get lost in the book she'd picked up in the gift shop. But she couldn't concentrate on the words long enough to make any progress. Time and again, her thoughts had returned to Nick. His face. His eyes. The cool dismissal on his face when he'd first seen the pictures of their sons.

She didn't know what was coming next, and the worry over it had gnawed at her insides all day. Which was why she'd decided to keep her margarita date with Mary. Jenna had spent too much time alone today, with too much time for thinking. What she needed now was some distraction. A little tequila-flavored relaxation sounded great. Especially since she had dinner with Nick to look forward to.

"Oh God," she whispered as her stomach fisted into knots again.

"Jenna!"

A woman's voice called out to her, and Jenna turned in that direction. She spotted Mary, standing up at one of the tables along the wall, waving and smiling at her. Gratefully Jenna headed her way, threading a path through the milling crowd. When she reached the table, she slid onto a chair and smiled at the margarita already waiting for her.

"Hope you don't mind. I ordered one for you as soon as I got here," Mary told her, taking a big gulp of her own oversize drink.

"Mind?" Jenna said, reaching for her frosty glass, "Are you kidding? This is fabulous." When she'd taken a long, deep gulp of the icy drink, she sat back and looked at her new friend.

Mary was practically bouncing in her seat, and her eyes were shining with excitement. Her blond hair looked wind tousled and her skin was a pale red, as if she'd had plenty of sun today. "I've been looking for you all over this ship," she said, grinning like a loon. "I had to see you. Find out where they put you."

Jenna blinked and shook her head. "What do you mean? Put me? Where *who* put me?"

Mary stretched one hand out and grabbed Jenna's for a quick squeeze. "Oh my God. You haven't been back down to the pit all day, have you?"

"No way," Jenna said on a sigh. "After my meeting, I came topside and I've been putting off going back down by hanging out on the Verandah Deck."

"So you don't know."

"Know what?" Jenna was beginning to think that maybe Mary had had a few margaritas too many. "What're you talking about?"

"It's the most incredible thing. I really can't believe it myself and I've seen it." She slapped one hand to her pale blue blouse and groaned like she was in the midst of an orgasm.

"Mary…what is going on?"

"Right, right." The blonde picked up her drink, took a big gulp and said, "It happened early this afternoon. Joe and I were up on the Promenade, you know, looking at all the shops. Well," she admitted, "I was looking, Joe was being dragged reluctantly along behind me. And when we came out of the Crystal Candle—which you should really check out, they have some amazing stuff in there—"

Jenna wondered if there was a way to get Mary to stay on track long enough to tell her what was happening. But probably not, so she took a sip of her drink and prepared to wait it out. She didn't have to wait long.

"When we came out," Mary was saying, "there was a ship steward waiting for us. He said, 'Mr. and Mrs. Curran?' all official-sounding and for a second I wondered what we'd done wrong, but we hadn't done anything and so Joe says, 'What's this about?' and the steward only told us to go with him."

"Mary…"

Her new friend grinned. "I'm getting to it. Really. It's just that it's all so incredible—right." She waved one hand to let Jenna know she was back on track, then she went right back to her story. "The steward takes us up to the owner's suite—you know, Nick Falco?"

"Yeah," Jenna murmured. "I know who he is."

"Who in the English-speaking world doesn't?" Mary said on a laugh, then continued. "So we're standing there in the middle of a suite that looks like a palace or something and Nick Falco himself comes up to us, introduces himself and *apologizes* about our cabin in the pit."

"What?" Jenna just stared at the other woman, not sure what to make of all this.

"I know! I was completely floored, let me tell you. I was almost speechless and Joe can tell you that that almost never happens." She paused for another gulp of her drink and when she finished it, held up one hand for the waitress to bring another. "So there we are and Mr. Falco's being so nice and so sincere about how he feels so badly about the state of the rooms on the Riviera Deck—and can you believe how badly misnamed that deck is?—and he *insists* on upgrading us."

"Upgrading?"

"Seriously upgrading," Mary said as she thanked the waitress for her fresh margarita. She waited until the server had disappeared with her empty glass before continuing. "So I'm happy, because hey, that tiny cabin is just so hideous. And I'm expecting a middle-grade cabin with maybe a porthole, which would be *great*. But that's not what we got."

"It's not?" Jenna set her glass down onto the table and watched as Mary's eyes actually sparkled even harder than they had been.

"Oh, no. Mr. Falco said that most of the cabins were already full, which is how we got stuck in those tiny ones in the first place. So he moved us into a *luxury suite!*"

"He did?"

"It's on the Splendor Deck. The same level as Mr. Falco's himself. And Jenna, our suite is amazing! It's bigger than my *house*. Plus, he said our entire cruise is on him. He's refunding what we paid for that hideous cabin and insisting that we pay *nothing* on this trip."

"Wow." Nick had always taken great pride in keeping his passengers happy, but this was…well, to use Mary's word, *amazing*. Cruise passengers usually looked forward to a bill at the end of a cruise that could amount to several hundred dollars. Oh, the food and accommodations were taken care of when you rented your cabin. But incidentals could really pile up on a person if they weren't paying attention.

By doing this, Nick had given Mary and her husband a cruising experience that most people would never know. Maybe there was more heart to the man than she'd once believed.

"He's just so nice," Mary was saying, stirring her slender straw through the icy confection of her margarita. "Somehow, I thought a man that rich and that famous and that playboylike would be sort of...I don't know, snotty. But he wasn't at all. He was really thoughtful and kind, and I can't believe this is all really happening."

"It's terrific, Mary," Jenna said sincerely. Even if she and Nick had their problems, she could respect and admire him for what he'd done for these people.

"I'm really hoping your upgrade will have you somewhere near us, Jenna. Maybe you should go and see a steward about it, find out where they're moving you."

"Oh," Jenna said with a shake of her head, "I don't think I'll be moving." She couldn't see Nick doing her any favors. Not with the hostility that had been spilled between them only a few hours ago. And though she was happy for Mary and her husband, Jenna wasn't looking forward to being the only resident on the lowest deck of the ship. Now it would not only be small and dark, but small and dark and creepy.

"Of course you will," Mary countered. "They wouldn't move us and *not* you. That wouldn't make any sense at all."

Jenna just smiled. She wasn't about to go into her past history with Nick at the moment. So there was nothing she could really say to her new friend, other than, "I'll find out when I go downstairs to change. I've got a dinner appointment in about," she checked her wristwatch, "an hour and a half. So let's just have our drinks and you can tell me all about your new suite before I have to leave."

Mary frowned briefly, then shrugged. "Okay, but if you haven't been upgraded, I'm going to be really upset."

"Don't be." Jenna smiled and, to distract her, asked, "Do you have a balcony?"

"Two!" Mary crowed a little, grinned like a kid on Christmas morning and said, "Joe and I are going to have dinner on one of them tonight. Out under the stars...mmm. Time for a little romance now that we're out of the pit!"

Romance.

As Mary talked about the plans she and her husband had made for a night of seduction, Jenna smiled. She wished her friend well, but as for herself, she'd tried romance and had gotten bitten in the butt for her trouble. Nope, she was through with the hearts-and-flowers thing. All she wanted now was Nick's assurance that he would do the right thing and allow her to raise her sons the way she wanted to.

Her cabin was locked.

"What the—" Jenna slid her key card into the slot, whipped it out again and...nothing. The red light on the lock still shone as if it was taunting her. She knew it wouldn't do any good, but still, she grabbed the door handle and twisted it hard before shaking it, as if she could somehow convince the damn thing to open for her.

But nothing changed.

She glanced over her shoulder at what had been the Curran cabin, but no help would be found there. The happy couple were comfortably ensconced in their floating palace. "Which is all fine and good for *them*," Jenna muttered. "But what about *me?*"

Giving up, she turned around, leaned back against her closed door and looked up and down the narrow, dark corridor. This was just great. Alone in the pit. No way to call for help. She'd have to go back topside and find a ship phone.

"Perfect. Just perfect." Her head was a little swimmy from the margaritas and her stomach was twisted in knots of expectation over the upcoming dinner with Nick, and now she couldn't even take a shower and change clothes. "This is going so well."

She stabbed the elevator button and when the door opened instantly, she stepped inside. The Muzak pumping through the speakers was a simply hideous orchestral rendition of "Stairway to Heaven" and didn't do a thing to calm her down.

Jenna exited onto the Promenade Deck and was instantly swallowed by the crowd of passengers wandering around the shops. The lobby area was done in glass and wood with a skylight installed in the domed ceiling overhead that displayed a blue summer sky studded with white, puffy clouds.

But she wasn't exactly on a sightseeing mission. She plowed through the crowd to a booth where one of Nick's employees stood ready to help passengers with answers to their questions. The man in the red shirt and white slacks wearing a name tag that read Jeff gave Jenna a welcoming smile as he asked, "How can I help you?"

She tried not to take her frustration out on him. After all, he was trying to help. "Hi, I'm Jenna Baker, and I'm in cabin 2A on the Riviera deck and—"

"Jenna Baker?" he interrupted her quickly, frowned a little, then checked a clipboard on the desk in front of him.

"Yes," she said, attempting to draw his attention back to her. "I just came from my cabin and my key card didn't work, so—"

"Ms. Baker," he said, his attitude changing from flirtatious and friendly to crisp professionalism. "There's a notation here asking that you be escorted to the Splendor Deck."

Where Mary's new cabin was. So Nick had upgraded Jenna, as well? Unexpected and frankly, a relief. A suite would be much more comfortable than the closet she'd been assigned.

But… "All of my things are still in my cabin, so I really need to get in there to pack and—"

"No, ma'am," Jeff said quickly, smiling again. "Your cabin was packed up by the staff and your luggage has already been moved. If you'll just take that elevator—" he paused to point at a bank of elevators opposite them "—to the Splendor Deck, you'll be met and directed to your new cabin."

Strange. She didn't know how she felt about someone else rooting through her things, but if it meant she could get into a shower, change clothes and get ready for her meeting with Nick, then she'd go with it. "Okay then, and, um, thanks."

"It's a pleasure, Ms. Baker. I hope you enjoy your stay with Falcon Cruises."

"Uh-huh." She waved distractedly and headed for the elevators. Not much chance of her enjoying her cruise when she was here to do battle with the King of Cruise Lines. Nope, the most she could hope for was getting out of the pit and into a nicer cabin courtesy of one Mr. Nick Falco.

When the elevator stopped on the Splendor Deck, Jenna stepped out into a wide, lushly carpeted hallway. The ceiling was tinted glass, open to the skies but dark enough to keep people from frying in direct sunlight. The walls were the color of rich cream and dotted with paintings of tropical islands, ships at sea and even simple ocean scenes with whitecaps that looked real enough to wet your fingers if you reached out to touch them.

The one thing she didn't see was someone to tell her where to go now that she was here. But almost before that thought formed in her mind, Jenna heard the sound of footsteps hurrying toward her. She turned and buried her surprise when she recognized Teresa Hogan, Nick's assistant.

"Jenna. It's good to see you," the older woman said, striding to her with long, determined steps. Her smile looked real, her sharp green eyes were warm and when she reached out a hand in welcome, Jenna was happy to take it.

"Nice to see you, too, Teresa." They'd met during that magical week with Nick more than a year ago.

Ordinarily, as just an assistant to the cruise director, Jenna never would have come into contact with the big boss's righthand woman. But as the woman having an affair with Nick, Jenna'd met Teresa almost right away.

Teresa had been friendly enough, until the truth about Jenna being one of Nick's employees had come out. Then the coolly efficient Teresa had drawn a line in the sand, metaphorically speaking. She chose to defend Nick and make sure Jenna never had the chance to get near him again.

At the time, it had made Jenna furious, now she could understand that loyalty. And even appreciate it in a way.

"How've you been?" Jenna smiled as she asked, determined to keep the friendly tone that Teresa had begun.

"Busy." The older woman shrugged. "You know the boss. He keeps us hopping."

"Yes," Jenna mused. "He always did."

A long, uncomfortable moment passed before Teresa said, "So, you know about the cabins on the Riviera Deck being sealed."

"That's why I'm here," Jenna said, shooting a glance up and down the long, empty hallway. "I saw Mary Curran earlier, she told me she and her husband had been upgraded. And then I went to my cabin and couldn't get in. Jeff at information sent me here."

"Good." Teresa nodded and her short, dark hair didn't so much as dip with the movement. She pointed behind Jenna to the end of the wide, plush hall. "The Currans' suite is right along there. And now if you'll come with me, I'll take you to your new cabin. We can talk as we go."

They headed off in the opposite direction of the Currans'. Walking toward the bow of the great ship, Jenna casually glanced at the artwork as she passed it and tried to figure out what was going on. Being escorted by the owner's assistant seemed unusual. Shouldn't a steward have been put in charge of seeing her to her new accommodations? But did it really matter? Jenna followed along in Teresa's wake, hurrying to keep up with the woman who seemed always to be in high gear.

"You can imagine," Teresa said over her shoulder, "that Nick was appalled to find out the cabins on the lowest deck had been rented."

"Appalled, huh?" Jenna rolled her eyes. Clearly Teresa was still faithful to the boss. "Then why rent them at all?"

Teresa's steps hitched a little as she acknowledged, "It was a mistake. The cabins below were supposed to have been sealed before leaving port for this maiden voyage. The person responsible for going against the boss's orders was reprimanded."

"Shot at dawn? Or just fired without references?" Jenna asked in a low-pitched voice.

Teresa stopped dead and Jenna almost ran right into her.

"Nick doesn't fire indiscriminately and you know it." Teresa lifted her chin pointedly as she moved to protect her boss. "*You* lied to him. That's why you were fired, Jenna."

A flush stole through her. Yes, she'd lied. She hadn't meant to, but that's what had happened. And she hadn't been able to find a way out of the lie once it had begun. Still, he might have listened to her once the bag was open and the cat was out.

"He could have let me explain," Jenna argued and met that cool green stare steadily.

Just for an instant the harsh planes of Teresa's expression softened a bit. She shook her head and blew out a breath. "Look, Nick's not perfect—"

"Quite the admission coming from you."

Teresa smiled tightly. "True. I do defend him. I do what I can to help him. He's a good boss. And he's been good to me. I'm not saying that how he handled the… situation with you was right—"

Jenna stopped her, holding up both hands. "You know what? Never mind. It was more than a year ago. It's over and done. And whatever Nick and I had has ended, too."

Teresa cocked her head to one side and looked at her thoughtfully. "You really think so, hmm?"

"Trust me on this," Jenna said as they started walking again. "Nick is *so* over me."

"If you say so." Teresa stopped in front of a set of double doors. Waving one hand at them as if she were a game show hostess displaying a brand-new refrigerator, she said, "Here we are. Your new quarters. I hope you like them."

"I'm sure they'll be great. Way better than the Riviera Deck anyway."

"Oh," Teresa said with a smile, "that's certainly a fair

statement. You go on in, your things have been un-packed. I'm sure I'll be seeing you again."

"Okay." Jenna stood in the hall and watched as Teresa strode briskly down the long hallway. There was something going on here, she thought, she just couldn't quite puzzle it out yet.

Then she glanced at her wristwatch, saw she had less than an hour to get ready for her dinner with Nick and opened the door with the key card Teresa had given her.

She walked inside, took a deep breath and almost genuflected.

The room was incredible—huge, and sprawlingly spacious, with glass walls that displayed a view of the ocean that stretched out into infinity. The wide blue sky was splashed with white clouds and the roiling sea re-flected that deep blue back up at it.

Pale wood floors shone with an old gold gleam and the furniture scattered around the room looked designed for comfort. There was a fireplace on one wall, a wet bar in the corner and what looked to be priceless works of art dotting the walls. There were vases filled with glorious arrangements of fresh flowers that scented the air until she felt as if she were walking in a garden.

"This can't be my cabin," Jenna whispered, whip-ping her head from side to side as she tried to take in everything at once. "Okay, sure, upgraded to a suite. But this is the Taj Mahal of suites. There has to be a mistake, that's all."

"There's no mistake," Nick said as he walked easily into the room and gave her a smile that even from across the room was tempting enough to make her gasp. "This is my suite and it's where you'll be staying."

Four

"You can't be serious." Jenna took one instinctive step back, but couldn't go anywhere unless she turned, opened the door and sprinted down that long hallway.

"Damn serious," he said, and walked toward her like a man with all the time in the world.

He wore a dark blue, long-sleeved shirt, open at the collar, sleeves rolled back to his elbows. His black slacks had a knife-sharp crease in them, and his black shoes shone. But it was his eyes that held her. That pale blue gaze fixed on her as if he could see straight through her. As if he were looking for all of her secrets and wouldn't give up the quest until he had them.

"Nick, this is a bad idea," she said, and silently congratulated herself on keeping her tone even.

"Why's that?" He spread both hands out and shrugged. "You came to my boat. You tell me I'm the father of your children and insist we have to talk. So now you're here. We can talk."

Talk. Yeah.

In a floating palace that looked designed for seduction. Meeting Nick in her tiny cabin hadn't exactly been easy, but at least down there, there'd been no distractions. No easy opulence. No sensory overload of beauty.

This was a bad idea. Jenna knew it. Felt it. And didn't have a single clue how to get out of it.

"We shouldn't be staying together," she said finally, and winced because even to her she sounded like a prissy librarian or something.

"We'll be staying in the same cabin. Not together. There's a difference." He was so close now all he had to do was reach out and he could touch her.

If he did, she'd be a goner though, and she knew it.

"What's the matter, Jenna?" he asked. "Don't trust yourself alone with me?"

"Oh, please." She choked out a half laugh that she desperately hoped sounded convincing. "Could you get over yourself for a minute here?"

He gave her a slow smile that dug out the dimple in his left cheek and lit wicked lights in his eyes. Jenna's stomach flip-flopped and her mouth went dry.

"I'm not the one having a problem."

Did he have to smell so good?

"No problem," she said, lifting her chin and forcing

herself to look him dead in the eye. "Trust me when I say all I want from you is what your kids deserve."

The smile on Nick's face faded away as her words slammed home. Was he a father? Were those twin boys his? He had to know. To do that, he needed some time with Jenna. He needed to talk to her, figure out what she was after, make a decision about where to go from here.

Funny, Nick had been waiting all afternoon to enjoy that look of stunned disbelief on Jenna's face when she first walked into his suite and realized that she'd be staying with him. Payback for how he must have looked when he'd first seen the photo of the babies she claimed were his sons. But he hadn't enjoyed it as much as he'd thought. Because there were other considerations. Bigger considerations.

His sons. Nick's insides twisted into knots that were beginning to feel almost familiar. Countless times during the day, he'd looked at the photo of the babies he still carried in his shirt pocket. Countless times he'd asked himself if it was really possible that he was a father.

And though he wasn't prepared to take Jenna's word for his paternity, he had to admit that it wasn't likely she'd have come here to the ship, signing up for a cruise if it wasn't true. Not that he thought she'd have any qualms about lying—she'd lied to him when she first met him after all—but *this* lie was too easily found out.

So he was willing to accept the possibility. Which left him exactly where? *That* was the question that had been circling in his mind all afternoon, and he was no closer to an answer now than he had been earlier.

He looked her up and down and could admit at least to himself that she looked damn good to him. Her dark blond hair was a little windblown, stray tendrils pulling away from her braid to lay against her face. Her eyes were wide and gleaming with suspicion, and, strangely enough, that didn't do a damn thing to mitigate the attraction he felt as he drew in a breath that carried her scent deep into his lungs.

"I'll stay here, but I'm not sleeping with you," she announced suddenly.

Nick shook his head and smiled. "Don't flatter yourself. I said you're staying in my suite, not my bed. As it happens, there are three bedrooms here besides my own. Your things have been unpacked in one of them."

She frowned a little and the flush of color in her cheeks faded a bit. "Oh."

"Disappointed?" Nick asked, feeling a quick jolt of something hot and reckless punch through him.

"Please," she countered quickly. "You're not exactly irresistible, Nick."

He frowned at that, but since he didn't actually believe her, he let it go.

"I'm actually grateful to be out of that hole at the bottom of the ship," she added, glancing around at the suite before shifting her gaze back to his. "And if staying here is the price I have to pay for your attention, then I'll pay."

One dark eyebrow lifted. "How very brave of you to put up with such appalling conditions as these."

"Look," Jenna told him, "if you don't mind, it's been

a long day. So how about you just tell me which room is mine so I can take a shower. Then we'll talk."

"Fine. This way." He turned, pointed and said, "Down that hall. First door on the left."

"Thanks."

"My bedroom's at the end of the hall on the right."

She stopped, looked back at him over her shoulder and said, "I'll make a note."

"You do that," he whispered as she left the room, shoulders squared, chin lifted, steps long and slow, as if she were being marched to her death.

His gaze dropped to the curve of her behind and something inside him stirred into life. Something he hadn't felt since the last time he'd seen Jenna. Something he'd thought he was long past.

He still wanted her.

Spinning around, Nick stalked across the room to the wide bank of windows that displayed an awe-inspiring view of the sea. His gaze locked on the horizon as he fought to control the raging tide of lust rising inside him.

Jenna Baker.

She'd turned him inside out more than a year ago. Ever since, he'd been haunted by memories of their time together until he wasn't sure if what he was remembering was real or just fevered imaginings offered by a mind that couldn't seem to let go of the woman who'd lied to him. And Nick wasn't a man to forget something like that. Now she was back again. Here, trapped on his ship in the middle of the ocean with nowhere to go to escape him.

Yes, they had plenty to talk about—and if her children were indeed his sons, then there were a lot of decisions to be made. But, he told himself as he shoved both hands into his slacks pockets and smiled faintly at the sunlight glinting on the vast expanse of the sea, there would be enough time for him to have her again.

To feel her under him. To lay claim to her body once more. To drive her past the edge of reason. Then, when he was satisfied that he'd gotten her out from under his skin, he'd kick her loose and she'd be out of his life once and for all. He wouldn't even allow her to be a memory this time.

In Neptune's Garden, the elegant restaurant on the Splendor Deck, Jenna watched as Nick worked the room.

As the owner of the ship, he wasn't exactly expected to mingle with the passengers, but Nick was an executive like no other. He not only mingled, he seemed to enjoy himself. And with her arm tucked through his, Jenna felt like a queen moving through an adoring crowd.

Again and again, as they walked to their table, Nick stopped to chat with people sitting at the white linen–covered tables. Making sure they were enjoying the ship, asking if there was anything they needed and didn't have, if there was anything that the crew could do to make their stay more pleasurable.

Of course the single women on board were more than anxious to meet the gorgeous, wealthy, eligible Nick Falco. And the fact that Jenna was on his arm didn't dissuade them from flirting desperately.

"It's a beautiful ship, Mr. Falco," one woman said with a sigh as she shook his hand. She tossed her thick black hair back over her shoulder and licked her lips.

"Thank you," he said, smiling at her and the two other women seated with her. "I'm happy you're enjoying yourselves. If there's anything you need, please be sure to speak to a steward."

"Oh," the brunette cooed, "we will. I promise."

Jenna just managed to keep from rolling her eyes. All three women were looking at Nick as if he were the first steak they'd stumbled on after leaving a spa dinner of spinach leaves and lemon slices. And he was eating it up, of course.

When he turned to go, he led her on through the crowd and Jenna swore she could feel the death stare from those women boring into her back.

"Well, that was tacky," she murmured.

"Tacky?"

"The way she practically drooled on you."

"Ah," Nick said, flashing a quick grin at her as he opened his right hand—the hand the brunette had shaken and clung to. A cabin key card rested in the center of his palm and the number P230 was scrawled across the top in ink. "So I'm guessing this makes it even tackier."

"Oh, for God's sake," Jenna snapped, wanting to spin around and shoot a few daggers at the brunette with no class. "I was *with* you. For all she knew I was your girlfriend."

His pale blue eyes sparkled and his grin widened

enough that the dimple in his left cheek was a deep cleft. "Jealous?"

She tried to pull her hand free of the crook of his arm, but he held her tight. Frowning, she said, "No. Not jealous. Just irritated."

"By her? Or by me?"

"A little of both." She tipped her head back to look up at him. "Why didn't you give the key back to her?"

He looked genuinely surprised at the suggestion. "Why would I embarrass her in front of her friends?"

Jenna snorted indelicately. "I'm guessing it's next to impossible to embarrass a woman like *that*."

"This really bothers you."

It always had, she thought. When she first went to work for Falcon Cruise Lines, she'd heard all the stories. About how on every cruise there were women lining up to take their place in Nick's bed. He was a player, no doubt. But for some reason, Jenna had allowed herself to be swept up in the magic of the moment. She'd somehow convinced herself that what they'd had together was different from what he found with countless other women.

Apparently, she'd been wrong about a few things.

"One question," she said, keeping her voice low enough that no one they passed could possibly overhear.

"Okay."

"Are you planning on using that key?"

He only looked at her for a long moment or two, then sighing, he stopped a waiter, handed over the key card and whispered something Jenna didn't quite catch. Then he turned to her. "That answer your question?"

"Depends," she said. "What did you tell him?"

"To return the card to the brunette with my thanks and my regrets."

A small puddle of warmth settled in Jenna's chest and even though she knew it was foolish, she couldn't quite seem to quash it. "Thank you."

He dipped his head in a faint mockery of a bow. "I find there's only one woman I'm interested in talking to at the moment."

"Nick…"

"Here we are," he said, interrupting whatever she would have said as he seated her in the navy blue leather booth that was kept reserved for him. "Jenna, let's have some dinner and get started on that talk you wanted."

Jenna slid behind the linen-draped table and watched him as he moved around to take a seat beside her. "All right, Nick. First let me ask you something, though."

"What?"

"All the people you talked to as we came through the restaurant…all the women you flirted with…" Jenna shook her head as she looked at him. "You haven't changed a bit, have you?"

His features tightened as he looked at her, and in the flickering light of the single candle in the middle of their table, his eyes looked just a little dangerous. "Oh, I've changed some," he told her softly, and the tone of his voice rippled across her skin like someone had spilled a glass of ice water on her. "These days I'm a little more careful who I spend time with. I don't take a woman's word for it anymore when she tells me who she is. Now

I check her out. Don't want to run across another liar, after all."

Jenna flushed. She felt the heat of it stain her skin and she was grateful for the dim lighting in the restaurant. Folding her hands together in her lap, she looked at the snowy expanse of the table linen and said, "Okay, I'm going to say this again. I didn't set out to lie to you back then, Nick."

"So it just happened?"

"Well," she said, lifting her gaze reluctantly to his, "yes."

"Right." He nodded, gave her a smirk that came nowhere near being a real smile and added, "Couldn't figure out a way to tell me that you actually worked for me, so you just let it slide. Let me think you were a passenger."

Yes, she had. She'd been swept away by the moonlight and the most gorgeous man she'd ever seen in her life. "I never said I was. You assumed I was a passenger."

"And you said nothing to clear that up."

True. All true. If she'd simply told the truth, then their week together never would have happened. She never would have known what it was like to be in his arms. Never would have imagined a future of some kind between them. Never would have gotten pregnant. Never would have given birth to the two little boys she couldn't imagine living without.

Because of that, it was hard to feel guilty about what she'd done.

"Nick, let's not rehash the past, all right? I said I

was sorry at the time. I can't change anything. And you know, you didn't exactly act like Prince Charming at the time, either."

"You're blaming me?"

"You wouldn't even talk to me," she reminded him. "You found out the truth and shut me out and down so fast I was half surprised you didn't have me thrown overboard to swim home."

He shifted uncomfortably, worked his jaw as if words were clamoring to get out and he was fighting the impulse to shout them. "What did you expect me to do?"

"All I wanted was to explain myself."

"There was nothing you could have said."

"Well," she said softly, "we'll never know for sure, will we?" Then she sighed and said, "We're not solving anything here, so let's just let the past go, okay? What happened, happened. Now we need to talk about what *is*."

"Right." He signaled to a waiter, then looked at her again. "So let's talk. Tell me about your sons."

"*Your* sons," she corrected, lifting her chin a little as if readying to fight.

"That's yet to be proved to me."

"Why would I lie?"

"Hmm. Interesting question," he said. "I could say you've lied before, but then we've already agreed not to talk about the past."

Jenna wasn't sure if she wanted to sigh in frustration or kick him hard under the table. This was so much more difficult than she'd thought it would be. Somehow,

Jenna had convinced herself that Nick would believe her. That he would look at the pictures of the babies and somehow *know* instinctively that these were his sons. She should have known better.

All around them the clink of fine crystal and the muted conversations of the other diners provided a background swell of sound that was more white noise than anything else. Through the windows lining one side of the restaurant, the night was black and the sea endless. The shimmer of colored lights hanging from the edges of the deck looked almost like a rainbow that only shone at night.

And beside her, the man who'd haunted her dreams and forged a new life for her sat waiting, watchful.

As she started to speak, a waiter approached with a bottle of champagne nestled inside a gleaming silver bucket. Jenna closed her mouth and bit her lip as the waiter poured a sip of the frothy wine into a flute and presented it to Nick for tasting. Approved, the wine was then poured first for her, then for Nick. Once the waiter had disappeared into the throng again, Jenna reached for her champagne and took a sip, hoping to ease the sudden dryness in her throat.

"So?" Nick prodded, his voice a low rumble of sound that seemed to slide inside her. "Tell me about the twins."

"What do you want to know?"

He shot her a look. "Everything."

Nodding, Jenna took a breath. Normally, she was more than happy to talk about her sons. She'd even been known to bore complete strangers in the grocery store with tales of their exploits. But tonight was different. Important. This was the father of her children. She had to make him understand that. Believe it. So choosing her words carefully, she started simply and said, "Their names are Jacob and Cooper."

He frowned a little and took a sip of his own champagne. "Family names?"

"My grandfathers," she said, just a touch defensively as if she was prepared to go toe to toe with him to guard her right to name her sons whatever she wanted.

"That was nice of you," he said after a second or two and took the wind out of her sails. "Go on."

While around them people laughed and talked and relaxed together, a tight knot of tension coiled about their table. Jenna's voice was soft, Nick leaned in closer to hear her and his nearness made her breath hitch in her chest.

"Jacob's sunny and happy all the time. He smiles from the minute he wakes up until the moment I put him down for the night." She smiled, too, just thinking of her babies. "Cooper's different. He's more…thoughtful, I guess. His smiles are rarer and all the more precious because of it. He's always watching. Studying. I'd love to know what he's thinking most of the time because even at four months, he seems almost a philosopher."

His gaze was locked on her and Jenna could see both of her sons in Nick's face. They looked so much like him, she couldn't understand how he could doubt even for a moment that they were his.

"Where are they now?"

"My sister Maxie's watching them." And was probably harried and exhausted. "The boys are crazy about her and she loves them both to death. They're fine."

"Then why did you get tense all of a sudden?"

She blew out a breath, slumped back against the booth and admitted, "It's the first time I've been away from them. It feels…wrong, somehow. And I miss them. A lot."

His eyes narrowed on her and he picked up his glass for a sip of wine. Watching her over the rim of the glass, he swallowed, then set the flute back onto the table. "Can't be easy, being a single mother."

"No, it's not," she admitted, thinking now about just how tired she was every night by the time she had the boys in bed. It had been so long since she'd been awake past eight o'clock at night that it was odd to her now, sitting here in a restaurant at nine. This was what it had been like before, though. When she'd only had herself to worry about. When she hadn't had two little boys depending on her.

God, how had she ever been able to stand the quiet? The emptiness in her little house? She couldn't even imagine being without her sons now.

"But," she added when he didn't say anything else, "along with all the work, a single mom gets all the perks to herself, too. I don't have to share the little moments. I'm the one to see them smile for the first time. To see them waking up to the world around them."

"So since you're not looking to share the good moments, that means you're not interested in having me involved in the twins' lives," he said thoughtfully. "All you really want is child support?"

She stiffened a little. Jenna hadn't even considered that Nick might want to be drawn into their sons' lives. He wasn't the hearth-and-home kind of guy. He was the party man. The guy you dated, but didn't bring home to mom.

"You and I both know you don't have any interest in being a father, Nick."

"Is that right? And how would you know that?"

"Well—"

He inclined his head at her speechlessness. "Exactly. You don't know me any more than I know you."

"You're wrong. I know that you're not the kind of man to tie himself down in one place. That week we were together you told me yourself you had no plans to ever get married and settle down."

"Who said anything about getting married?"

Jenna sucked in a breath and told herself to slow down. She was walking through a minefield here. "I didn't mean—"

"Forget it," he said.

Another waiter appeared, this time delivering a dinner that Nick had clearly ordered earlier. Surprised, Jenna looked down at the serving of breast of chicken and fettucine in mushroom sauce before lifting her gaze to his in question.

"I remembered you liked it," he said with a shrug.

What was she supposed to do with that? She wondered. He pretended to not care anything about her, yet he remembered more than a year later what her favorite foods were? Why? Why would he recall something so small?

Once the waiter was gone, Nick started talking again. "So answer me this. When you found out you were pregnant, why'd you go through with it?"

"Excuse me?"

He shrugged. "You were alone. A lot of women in that position wouldn't have done what you did. Giving birth, deciding to raise the babies on her own."

"They were mine," she said, as if that explained everything, and in her mind it did. Never for a moment had she considered ending her pregnancy. She'd tried to reach Nick of course, but when she couldn't, she'd hunkered down and started building a life for her and her children.

"No regrets?"

"Only the one about coming on this ship," she muttered.

He smiled faintly, laid his napkin across his lap and, picking up his knife and fork, sliced into his filet mignon. "I heard that."

"I meant you to." As Jenna used her fork to slide the fettucine noodles around her plate, she said, "Nick, my sons are the most important things in the world to me. I'll do whatever I have to to make sure they're safe."

"Good for you."

She took a bite of her dinner and, though she could tell it was cooked to perfection, the delicate sauce and chicken tasted like sawdust in her mouth.

"I'll want a DNA test."

"Of course," she said. "I've already had the boys' blood tests done at a local lab. You can send your sample in to them and they'll do the comparison testing."

"I'll take care of it tomorrow."

"What?" She shook her head, looked at him and said, "Don't you have to wait until we're back in San Pedro?"

"No, I'm not going to wait. I want this question settled as quickly as possible." He continued to eat, as though what they were discussing wasn't affecting him in the slightest. "We dock at Cabo in the morning. You and I will go ashore, find a lab and have them fax the findings to the lab in San Pedro."

"We will?" She hadn't planned on spending a lot of time with Nick, after all. She'd only come on board to tell him about the boys and frankly, she'd thought he wouldn't want anything more to do with her after that. Instead, he'd moved her into his suite and now was proposing that they spend even more time together.

"Until this is taken care of to my satisfaction," Nick told her softly, "I'm not letting you out of my sight. The two of us are going to be joined at the hip. So you might as well start getting used to it."

Five

Once the ship had docked and most of the passengers had disembarked for their day of shopping, sailing and exploring the city of Cabo San Lucas, Nick got busy. He'd already had Teresa make a few calls, and the lab at the local hospital was expecting them.

The sun was hot and bright and the scent of the sea greeted them the moment he and Jenna stepped out on deck. Ordinarily Nick would have been enjoying this. He loved this part of cruising. Docking in a port, exploring the city, revisiting favorite sites, discovering new ones.

But today was different. Today he was on a mission, so he wasn't going to notice the relaxed, party atmosphere of Cabo. Just as he wasn't going to notice the way Jenna's pale green sundress clung to her body or the way her legs looked in those high-heeled sandals. He had no interest in the fact that her dark blond hair looked like spilled honey as it flowed down over her shoulders and he really wasn't noticing her scent or the way it seemed to waft its way to him on the slightest breeze.

Having her stay in his suite had seemed like a good idea yesterday. But the knowledge that she was so close, that she was just down the hall from him, alone in her bed, had taunted him all night long. Now his eyes felt gritty, his temper was too close to the surface and his body was hard and achy.

Way to go, Falcon, he told himself.

"So where are we going?" she asked as he laid his hand at the small of her back to guide her down the gangplank to shore. Damn, just the tips of his fingers against her spine was enough to make him want to forget all about this appointment and drag her back to his cabin instead.

Gritting his teeth, he pushed that image out of his mind.

"Teresa called the hospital here," he muttered. "The lab's expecting us. They'll take a DNA sample, run it and fax the results to your lab. We should have an answer in a day or two."

She actually stumbled and he grabbed her arm in an instinctive move. "That fast?"

"Money talks," he said with a shrug. He'd learned long ago that with enough money, a man could accomplish anything. Way of the world. And for the first time, he was damned glad he was rich enough to demand fast action. Nick wanted this question of paternity settled.

Like now. He couldn't stop thinking about those babies. Couldn't seem to stop looking at the picture she'd given him of them.

Couldn't stop wondering how their very existence was going to affect—change—his life. So he needed to know if he was going to be a father or if he was simply going to be suing Jenna Baker for everything she had for lying to him. Again.

Her heels clicked against the gangway and sounded like a frantic heartbeat. He wondered if she was nervous. Wondered if she really was lying and was now worried about being found out. Had she thought he'd simply accept her word that her sons belonged to him? Surely not.

At the bottom of the gangway, a taxi was waiting. Silently blessing Teresa's efficiency, Nick opened the door for Jenna, and when she was inside, slid in after her. In short, sharp sentences spoken in nearly fluent Spanish, Nick told the driver where to go.

"I didn't know you spoke Spanish," she said as he settled onto the bench seat beside her.

"There's a lot about me you don't know," he said.

"I guess so."

Of course, the same could be said about what he knew of her. He remembered clearly their time together more than a year before. But in those stolen moments, he'd been more intent on burying himself inside her than discovering her thoughts, her hopes, her dreams. He'd told himself then that there would be plenty of time for them to discover each other. He couldn't have guessed that in one short week he'd find her, want her and then lose her.

Yet, even with the passion simmering between them, Nick could recall brief conversations when she'd talked about her home, her family. He'd thought at the time that she was different from the other women he knew. That she was more sincere. That she was more interested in *him,* the man, than she was in what he was. How much he had.

Of course, that little fantasy had been exploded pretty quickly.

He dropped into silence again as the cab took off. He didn't want to talk to her. Didn't want to think about anything but what he was about to do. With a simple check of his DNA, his life could be altered irrevocably forever. His chest was tight and his mind was racing. Cabo was no more than a colorful blur outside his window as they headed for the lab and a date with destiny.

In a few seconds the cab was swallowed by the bustling port city. At the dock and on the main drive that ran along the ocean, Cabo San Lucas was beautiful. The hotels, the restaurants and bars, everything was new and shone to perfection, the better to tempt the tourists who streamed into the city every year.

But just a few short blocks from the port and Cabo was a big city like any other. The streets were crowded with cars, and pedestrians leaped off the sidewalks and ran across the street with complete abandon, trusting that the drivers would somehow keep from running them down. Narrower, cobblestoned side streets spilled off the bigger avenues and from there came the tantalizing scents of frying onions, spices and grilling meat.

Restaurants and bars crowded together, their chipped stucco facades looking a little tattered as tourists milled up and down the sidewalks, cameras clutched in sunburned fists. As the cab driver steered his car through the maze of traffic, Nick idly glanced out the window and noted the open-air markets gathered together under dark green awnings. Under that umbrella were at least thirty booths where you could buy everything from turquoise jewelry to painted ceramic burros.

Cabo was a tourist town and the locals did everything they could to keep those vacation dollars in the city.

"Strange, isn't it?" she mused, and Nick turned his head to look at her. She was staring out her window at the city and he half wondered if she was speaking to him or to herself. "All of the opulence on the beach and just a few blocks away…"

"It's a city, like any other," he said.

She turned her head to meet his gaze. "It's just a little disappointing to see the real world beneath the glitz."

"There's always a hidden side. To everything. And everyone," he said, staring into her eyes, wondering what she was feeling. Wondering why he even cared.

"What's hidden beneath your facade, then?" she asked.

Nick forced a smile. "I'm the exception to the rule," he told her. "What you see is what you get with me. There are no hidden depths. No mysteries to be solved. No secrets. No lies."

Her features tightened slightly. "I don't believe that," she said. "You're not as shallow as you pretend to be, Nick. I remember too much to buy into that."

"Then your memory is wrong. Don't look for something that isn't there, Jenna," he said softly, just in case their driver spoke English. "I'm not a lonely rich boy looking for love." He leaned in toward her, keeping his gaze locked with hers, and added, "I'm doing this DNA test for my own sake. If those babies are mine, then I need to know. But I'm not the white-picket-fence kind of guy. So don't go building castles in the air. You'll get trapped in the rubble when they collapse."

Jenna felt a chill as she looked into those icy blue eyes of his. All night she'd lain in her bed, thinking about him, wondering if she'd done the right thing by coming to Nick. By telling him about their sons. Now she was faced with the very real possibility that she'd made a huge mistake.

Once he was convinced that the boys were his, then what? Would he really be satisfied with writing out a child support check every month? Or would he demand time with his children? And if he did, how would she fit him into their lives?

Picturing Nick spending time in her tiny house in Seal Beach was almost impossible. His lifestyle was so far removed from hers they might as well be from different planets.

"Nick," she said, "I know there's a part of you that thinks I'm lying about all of this. But I'm not." She paused, watched his reaction and didn't see a thing that made her feel any better, so she continued. "So, before you take this DNA test, I want you to promise me something."

He laughed shortly, but there wasn't a single spark of humor lighting his eyes. "Why would I do that?"

"No reason I can think of, but I'm still asking."

"What?" he asked, sitting back, dropping one hand to rest on his knee. "What's this promise?"

She tried again to read his expression, but his features were shuttered, closing her out so completely it was as if she were alone in the cab. But he was listening and that was something, she supposed.

"I want you to promise me that whatever happens, you won't take out what you feel for me on our sons."

He tipped his head to one side, studied her for a long moment or two, then as she held her breath, waiting for his response, he finally nodded. "All right. I give you my word. What's between you and me won't affect how I treat your sons."

Jenna gave him a small smile. "Thank you."

"But if they *are* my sons," he added quietly, "you and I have a lot of talking to do."

The DNA test was done quickly, and before she knew it, Jenna and Nick were back in the cab, heading for the docks again. Her stomach was churning as her mind raced, and being locked inside a car hurtling down a crowded street wasn't helping. She needed to walk. Needed to breathe. Needed to escape the trapped feeling that held her in a tight grip.

Turning to Nick, she blurted suddenly, "Can we get out? Walk the rest of the way to the dock?"

He glanced at her, and whatever he saw in her face must have convinced him because he nodded, then spoke to the driver in Spanish. A moment later the cab pulled to the curb. Jenna jumped out of the car as if she were on springs and took a deep breath of cool, ocean air while Nick paid their fare.

Tourists and locals alike crowded the sidewalk and streamed past her as if she were a statue. She tucked her purse under her left arm and turned her face into the breeze sliding down the street from the sea.

"It's still several blocks to the ship," Nick said as he joined her on the sidewalk. "You going to be able to make it in those shoes?"

Jenna glanced down at the heeled sandals she wore then lifted her gaze back to his. "I'll make it. I just— needed to get out of that cab and move around a little."

"I don't remember you being so anxious," he said.

She laughed a little and sounded nervous even to herself. "Not anxious, really. It's just that since the boys were born, I'm not used to being still. They keep me running all day long, and sitting in the back of that cab, I felt like I was in a cage or something and it didn't help that neither one of us was talking and we'd just come from the lab, so my brain was in overdrive and—"

He interrupted the frantic flow of words by holding up one hand. "I get it. And I could use some air, too. So why don't we start walking?"

"Good. That'd be good." God, she hadn't meant to go on a stream of consciousness there. If he hadn't stopped her, heaven only knew what would have come out of her mouth. As it was, he was looking at her like she was a stick of dynamite with a burning fuse.

He took her arm to turn her around, and the sizzle of heat that sprang up from his touch was enough to boil her blood and make her gasp for air. So not a good sign.

Music spilled from the open doorway of a cantina and a couple of drunk, college-age tourists stumbled out onto the sidewalk. Nick pulled Jenna tight against him and steered her past them, but when they were in the clear, he didn't release her. Not that she minded.

"So what's a typical day for you now?" he asked as they moved along the sidewalk, a part of, yet separate from, the colorful crowd of locals and tourists.

"Typical?" Jenna laughed in spite of the fact that every nerve ending was on fire and lit from within due to Nick's arm wrapped tightly around her waist. "I learned pretty quickly that with babies in the house there's no such thing as typical."

She risked a glance at him, and his blue eyes connected with hers for a heart-stopping second. Then he nodded and said, "Okay, then describe one of your untypical days for me."

"Well, for one thing, my days start a lot earlier than they used to," she said. "The twins sleep through the night now, thank God, but they're up and raring to go by six every morning."

"That can't be easy." His arm around her waist loosened a bit, but he didn't let her go and Jenna felt almost as if they were a real couple. Which was just dangerous thinking.

"No," she said quickly, to rein her imagination back in with cold, dry facts. Their lives were so different, he'd never be able to understand what her world was like. He woke up when he felt like it, had breakfast brought to his room and then spent the rest of his day wandering a plush cruise ship, making sure his guests were happy.

She, on the other hand...

"There are two diapers that need changing, two little bodies who need dressing and two mouths clamoring for their morning bottle. There are two cribs in the room they share and I go back and forth between them, sort of on autopilot." She smiled to herself as images of her sons filled her mind. Yes, it was a lot of work. Yes, she was tired a lot of the time. And no, she wouldn't change any of it.

"How do you manage taking care of two of them?"

"You get into a rhythm," she said with a shrug that belied just how difficult it had been to *find* that rhythm. "Cooper's more patient than his brother, but I try not to use that as an excuse to always take care of Jacob first. So, I trade off. One morning I deal with Cooper first thing and the next, it's Jacob's turn. I feed one, then the other and then get them into their playpen so I can start the first of the day's laundry loads."

"You leave them alone in a playpen?"

Instantly defensive, Jenna shot him a glare. "They're safe and happy and it's not as if I just toss them into a cage and go off to party. I'm right there with them. But I have to be able to get things done and I can't exactly leave them on the floor unattended, now, can I?"

"Hey, hey," he said, tightening his grip around her waist a little. "That wasn't a criticism…"

She gave him a hard look.

"Okay," he acknowledged, "maybe it was. But I didn't mean it to be. Can't be easy. A single mother with two babies."

"No, it's not," she admitted and her hackles slowly lowered. "But we manage. We have playtime and the two of them are so bright and so interested in everything…." She shook her head. "It's amazing, really, watching them wake up to the world a little more each day."

"Must be."

He was saying the right things, but his tone carried a diffidence she didn't much like. But then how could she blame him? He didn't believe yet that the boys were his sons. Of course, he would hold himself back, refusing to be drawn in until it had been proven to him that he was their father.

"When they take their naps, I work."

"Yeah," he said, guiding her around a pothole big enough to swallow them both, "you said you had your own business. What do you do?"

"Gift baskets," she said, lifting her chin a little. "I design and make specialty gift baskets. I have a few corporate clients, and I get a lot of business over the Internet."

"How'd you get into that?" he asked, and Jenna was almost sure he really was interested.

"I started out by making them up for friends. Birthdays, baby showers, housewarming, that sort of thing," she said. "It sort of took off from there. People started asking me to make them baskets, and after a while I realized I was running a business. It's great, though, because it lets me be home with the boys."

"And you like that."

Not a question, a statement. She stopped walking, looked up at him and said, "Yes, I like it. I couldn't bear the thought of the boys being in day care. I want to be the one to see all of their firsts. Crawling, walking, speaking. I want to hear their giggles and dry their tears. I want to be at the heart of their lives."

He studied her for a long minute or two, his gaze moving over her face as if he were trying to imprint her image on his mind. Or trying to read her thoughts to see if she had really meant everything she just said.

"Most women wouldn't want to be trapped in a house with two screaming babies all day," he finally said.

Instantly Jenna bristled. "*A*, the women you know aren't exactly the maternal type, now, are they? *B*, the boys don't scream all day and *C*, spending time with my kids isn't a trap. It's a gift. One I'm thankful for every single day. You don't know me, Nick. So don't pretend you do."

One dark eyebrow lifted, and an amused glint shone in those pale eyes of his. "I wasn't trying to insult you," he said softly. "I…admire what you're doing. What you feel for your sons. All I meant was, that what you said was nice to hear."

"Oh." Well, didn't she feel like an idiot? "I'm sorry. I guess I'm a little quick on the trigger."

"A little?" He laughed shortly, and started walking again, keeping his arm locked about her waist as if concerned she might wander off. "The words *Mother Grizzly* come to mind."

Even Jenna had to chuckle. "You're right, you know. I learned the moment the boys were born. I was so electrified just by looking at them…to know they'd come from me. It's an amazing feeling. Two tiny boys—one minute they're not there, and the next, they're breathing and crying and completely capturing my heart. I fell in love so completely, so desperately, that I knew instantly I would never allow anyone or anything to hurt them. *Nobody* criticizes my kids. Nobody."

"Yeah," he said, with a thoughtful look in his eyes. "I get it."

His hand at her waist flexed and his fingers began to rub gently, and through the thin fabric of her summery dress, Jenna swore she could feel his skin on hers. Her heartbeat jumped into high gear, and her breathing was labored. Meeting his gaze, she saw confusion written there and she had to ask, "What is it? What's wrong?"

Quickly he said, "Nothing. It's just…" He stopped, though, before he could explain. Then, shaking his head, he said, "Come on, we've still got a long walk ahead of us."

A half hour later Jenna's feet were aching and she was seriously regretting jumping out of that cab. But there were compensations, too. Such as walking beside Nick, his arm around her waist as if they were really a couple. She knew she should step out of his grasp, but truthfully, she was enjoying the feel of him pressed closely to her too much to do it.

It had been so long since their week together. And in the time since, she hadn't been with anyone else. Well, she'd been pregnant for a good part of that time, so not much chance of hooking up with someone new. But even if she hadn't been, she wouldn't have been looking. Nick had carved himself into her heart and soul in that one short week and had made it nearly impossible for her to think about being with anyone else.

Which was really too bad when she thought about it. Because he'd made it clear they weren't going to be getting together again. Not that she wanted that, or anything....

"Oh!" She stopped suddenly as they came abreast of the street market they'd passed on their way to the lab. An excellent way to clear her mind of any more disturbing thoughts of Nick. "Let's look in here."

Frowning some, like any man would when faced with a woman who wanted to shop, Nick said, "What could you possibly want to buy here? It's a tourist trap."

"That's what makes it fun," she told him, and slipped out of his grasp to walk beneath the awning and into the aisle that wound its way past at least thirty different booths.

She wandered through the crowd, sensing Nick's presence behind her. She glanced at tables set up with sterling silver rings and necklaces, leather coin purses and crocheted shawls that hung in colorful bunches from a rope stretched across the front of a booth. She smiled at the man selling tacos and ignored the rumbling of her stomach as she moved on to a booth selling T-shirts.

Nick came up behind her and looked over her head at the display of tacky shirts silk-screened with images of Cabo, sport fishing and the local cantinas. Shaking his head at the mystery that was women, he wondered why in the hell she'd chosen to shop here.

"Need a new wardrobe?" he asked, dipping his head so that his voice whispered directly into her ear.

She jumped a little, and he enjoyed the fact that he made her nervous. He'd felt it all day. That hum of tension simmering around her. When he touched her, he felt the heat and felt her response that fed the fires burning inside him. The moment he'd wrapped his arm around her waist, he'd known it was a mistake. But the feel of her body curved against his had felt good enough that he hadn't wanted to let her go.

Which irritated the hell out of him.

He'd learned his lesson with her a year ago. She'd lied to him about who she was. Who was to say she hadn't lied about her response to him? Wasn't lying still? But even as he thought that, he wondered if anyone could manufacture the kind of heat that spiraled up between them when their bodies brushed against each other.

"The shirts aren't for me," she was saying, and Nick pushed his thoughts aside to pay attention. "I thought maybe there'd be something small enough for the boys to—here!"

She pulled a shirt out from a stack and it was so

small, Nick could hardly believe that it could actually be worn. There was a grinning cartoon burro on the front and the words Baby Burros Need Love Too stenciled underneath it. "It's so cute! Don't you think so?"

Nick's breath caught hard in his chest as she turned her face up to his and smiled so brightly the shine in her eyes nearly blinded him. He'd given women diamonds and seen less of a display of joy. If this was an act, he thought, she should be getting an Oscar.

"Yeah," he said. "I guess it is." Then he looked past her to the woman who ran the booth and in Spanish told her they'd be needing two of the shirts.

Smiling, the woman found another matching shirt, dropped them both in a sack and held them out. Nick paid for the shirts before Jenna could dig in her purse. Then he took hold of her hand and, carrying the bag, led her back out onto the street.

"You didn't have to buy them," she told him once they were on their way to the dock again.

"Call it my first present to my sons."

She stumbled a little and he tightened his hold on her hand, steadying her even while he felt his own balance getting shaky.

"So you believe me?"

Nick felt a cold, hard knot settle into the pit of his stomach. He looked into Jenna's eyes and couldn't find the slightest sign of deception. Was she too good at hiding her secrets? Or were there no secrets to hide? Soon enough, he'd know for sure. But for now "I'm starting to."

Six

Three days later the ship docked in Acapulco.

"Oh, come on," Mary Curran urged, "come ashore with Joe and me. He's going scuba diving of all things, and I'd love some company while I spend all the money we saved by having this cruise comped."

Laughing, Jenna shook her head and sat back on the sofa in the living room of Nick's spectacular suite. "No, thanks. I think I'm going to stay aboard and relax."

Mary sighed in defeat. "How you can relax when you're staying in this suite with Nick Falco is beyond me. Heck, I've been married for twenty years and just looking at the guy gives me hot flashes."

Jenna knew just what her friend meant. For the past few days she and Nick had been practically in each other's pockets. They'd spent nearly every minute together, and when they were here in this suite, the spacious accommodations seemed to shrink to the size of a closet.

Jenna felt as if she were standing on a tight wire, uneasily balanced over a vat of lava. She was filled with heat constantly and knew that with the slightest wrong move, she could be immolated.

God, great imagery.

"Hello? Earth to Jenna?"

"Sorry." Jenna smiled, pushed one hand through her hair and blew out an unsteady breath. "Guess my mind was wandering."

"Uh-huh, and I've got a good idea where it wandered *to*."

"What?"

"Oh, honey, you've got it bad, don't you?" Mary leaned forward and squeezed Jenna's hand briefly.

Embarrassed and just a little concerned that Mary might be right, Jenna immediately argued. "I don't know what you mean."

"Sure you don't." Mary's smile broadened. "I say Nick's name and your eyes flash."

"Oh God…"

"Hey, what's the trouble? You're both single. And you're clearly attracted to each other. I mean, I saw Nick's face last night at dinner whenever he looked at you."

The four of them had had dinner together the night before, and though Jenna had been sure it would be an uncomfortable couple of hours—given the tension between her and Nick—they'd all had a good time. In fact, seeing Nick interacting with Joe Curran, hearing him laugh and tell stories about past cruises had really opened Jenna's eyes.

For so long, she'd thought of him only as a player. A man only interested in getting as many women as possible into his bed. A man who wasn't interested in anything that wasn't about momentary pleasure.

Now she'd seen glimpses of a different man. One who could enjoy himself with people who weren't members of the "celebrity crowd." A guy who could buy silly T-shirts for babies he wasn't even sure were his. A guy who could still turn her into a puddle of want with a glance.

"Do you want to talk about it?" Mary asked quietly.

Jenna took a long, deep breath and looked around the room to avoid meeting Mary's too-knowing gaze. Muted sunlight, diffused by the tinted glass, filled the room, creating shadows in the corners. It was quiet now, with Nick somewhere out on deck and the hum of the ship's powerful engines silenced while in port.

Shifting her gaze to Mary's, Jenna thought about spilling the whole story. Actually she could really use someone to talk to, and Mary had, in the past several days, already proven to be a good friend. But she couldn't get into it now. Didn't want to explain how she and Nick had come together, made two sons and then drifted apart. That was far too long a story.

"Thanks," she said, meaning it. "But I don't think so.

Anyway, you don't have time to listen. Joe will be waiting for you."

Mary frowned at her, but apparently realized that
Jenna didn't feel like talking. Standing up, she said,
"Okay, I'll go. But if you decide you need someone to
talk to…"

"I'll remember. Thanks."

Then Mary left and Jenna was alone. Alone with her
thoughts, racing frantically through her mind. Alone
with the desire that was a carefully banked fire deep
inside. Suddenly antsy, she jumped to her feet, crossed
the room and left the suite. She'd just go up on deck.
Sit in the sun. Try not to think. Try to relax.

The business of running a cruise line kept Nick moving from the time he got up until late at night. People
on the outside looking in probably assumed that he led
a life of leisure. And sure, there was still time for that.
But the truth was he had to stay on top of everything.
This cruise line was his life. The one thing he had. The
most important thing in the world to him. He'd worked
his ass off to get this far, to make his mark. And he
wasn't about to start slowing down now.

"If the band isn't working, contact Luis Felipe here
in town," he told Teresa, and wasn't surprised to see her
make a note on her PDA. "He knows all the local bands
in Acapulco. He could hook us up with someone who
could take over for the rest of the cruise."

The band they'd hired in L.A. was proving to be
more trouble than they were worth. With their rock star

attitudes, they were demanding all sorts of perks that hadn't been agreed on in their contracts. Plus, they'd been cutting short their last show of the evening because they said there weren't enough people in attendance to make it worthwhile. Not their call, Nick thought. They'd been hired to do a job, and they'd do it or they'd get off the ship in Mexico and find their own way home.

"Got it," Teresa said. "Want me to tell the band their days are numbered?"

"Yeah. We'll be in port forty-eight hours. Give 'em twenty-four to clean up their act—if they don't, tell 'em to pack their bags."

"Will do." She paused, and Nick turned to look at her. They were standing at the bow of the ship on the Splendor Deck, mainly because Nick hadn't felt like being cooped up in his office. And he couldn't go to his suite because Jenna was there. Being in the same room with her without reacting to her presence was becoming more of a challenge.

The last few days had been hell. Being with her every day, sleeping down the hall from her at night, knowing she was there, stretched out on a king-size bed, probably wearing what she used to—a tank top and a pair of tiny, bikini panties—had practically killed him. He'd taken more cold showers in the last three days than he had in the past ten years.

His plan to seduce Jenna and then lose her was backfiring. He was the one getting seduced. He was the one nearly being strangled with throttled-back desire. And he was getting damned sick of it. It was time to make a move. Time to take her to bed. Before they got the results of that DNA test.

Tonight, he decided. Tonight he'd have Jenna Baker back in his bed. Where he'd wanted her for the past year.

"Boss?"

He was almost surprised to hear Teresa's voice. Hell, he'd forgotten where the hell he was and what he was doing. Just thinking about Jenna had his body hard and aching.

"What is it?" He half turned away from the woman and hoped she wouldn't notice the very evident proof of just how hungry for Jenna he really was.

"The lab in Cabo called. They faxed the results of the DNA test to the lab in L.A."

"Good." His stomach fisted, but he willed it to loosen. Nothing to do about it now but wait for the results. Which would probably arrive by tomorrow. So, yeah. Tonight was the night.

"Do you want me to tell Jenna?"

Nick frowned at his assistant, then let the expression fade away. Wasn't her fault he felt like he was tied up in knots. "No, thanks. I'll do it."

"Okay." Teresa took a deep breath, held it, then blew it out. "Look, I know this is none of my business…"

"Never stopped you before," he muttered with a smile.

"No, I guess not," she admitted, swiping one hand through her wind-tousled hair. "So let me just say, I don't think Jenna's trying to play you."

He went perfectly still. From the shore came the sounds of car horns honking and a swell of noise that only a crowd of tourists released for the day could make. Waves slapped halfheartedly at the hull of the ship, and the wind whipped his hair into his eyes.

He pushed it aside as he looked at Teresa. "Is that right?"

She lifted her chin, squared her shoulders and looked him dead in the eye. "That's right. She's just not the type to do something like this. She never did give a damn about your money or who you were."

"Teresa—" He didn't want to talk about this and he didn't actually care what his assistant thought of Jenna. But knowing Teresa, there was just no way to stop her. An instant later, he was proved right.

"—still talking. And if I'm going to get fired for shooting my mouth off," she added quickly, "then I'm going to get it all said no matter what you think."

"Fine. Finish."

"I didn't say anything when you fired her, remember. I even agreed with you to a point—yes, Jenna should have told you she worked for you, but from her point of view I can see why she didn't."

"That's great, thanks."

She ignored his quips and kept talking. "I didn't even say anything when you were so miserable after she left that it was like working for a panther with one foot caught in a steel trap."

"Hey—"

"But I'm saying it now," she told him, and even wagged a finger at him as if he were a misbehaving ten-year-old. "You can fire me for it if you want to, but you'll never get another assistant as good as I am and you know it...."

Gritting his teeth because he knew she was right, Nick nodded and ordered, "Spit it out then."

"Jenna's not the kind to lie."

A bark of laughter shot from his throat.

"Okay, fine, she didn't tell you she was an employee. But that was one mistake. Remember, I knew her then, too, Nick. She's a nice kid with a good heart."

He shifted uncomfortably because he didn't want her to be right. It was much easier on him to think of Jenna as a liar and a manipulator. Those kind of women he knew how to deal with. A nice woman? What the hell was he supposed to do with one of those?

"*And,*" Teresa added pointedly, "I saw the pictures of your sons—"

"That hasn't been confirmed yet," he said quickly.

"They look just like you," she countered.

"All babies look like Winston Churchill," Nick argued, despite the fact that he knew damn well she was right.

"Yeah?" She smiled and shook her head. "Winston never looked that good in his life, I guarantee it. They've got your eyes. Your hair. Your dimples." Teresa paused, reached out and laid one hand on his forearm. "She's not lying to you, Nick. You're a father. And you're going to have to figure out how you want to deal with that."

He turned his face toward the sea and let the wind slap at him. The wide stretch of openness laid out in front of him was usually balm enough to calm his soul and soothe whatever tensions were crowded inside him. But it wasn't working now. And maybe it never would again.

Because if he was a father…then his involvement with those kids wasn't going to be relegated to writing a check every month. He'd be damned if his children were going to grow up not knowing him. Whether Jenna wanted him around or not, he wasn't going anywhere. He was going to be a part of their lives, even if that meant he had to take them away from their mother to do it.

The ship felt deserted.

With most of the passengers still on shore exploring Acapulco, Jenna wandered decks that made her feel as if she were on board a ghost ship. That evening, she was back in Nick's suite and feeling on edge. She'd showered, changed into a simple, blue summer dress and was now fighting the fidgets as she waited for Nick to come back to the suite for dinner.

Funny, she'd spent nearly every waking moment with him over the past few days, feeling her inner tension mount incrementally. She'd convinced herself that what she needed was time to herself. Time away from Nick, to relax. Unwind a little, before the stress of being so close to him made her snap.

So she'd had that time to herself today and she was more tense than ever.

"Oh, you're in bad shape, Jenna," she whispered as she walked out onto Nick's balcony. She was a wreck when she was with him, and when she wasn't, she missed him. Her hair lifted off her neck in the wind, and the hem of her dress fluttered about her knees. Her sandals made a soft click of sound as she walked across the floor and she wrapped her arms around herself more for comfort than warmth.

From belowdecks, a soft sigh of music from the ballroom reached her, and the notes played on the cool ocean breeze, as if they'd searched her out deliberately. The plaintive instrumental seeped into her soul and made her feel wistful. What if coming on this trip had been a big mistake? What if telling Nick about their sons hadn't been the right thing to do? What if—she stopped her wildly careening thoughts and told herself it was too late to worry about any of that now. The deed was done. What would happen would happen and there wasn't a damn thing she could do about it now.

She sighed, leaned on the balcony railing and stared out at the sea. Moonlight danced on the surface of the water in a shimmer of pale silver. Clouds scuttled across a star-splashed sky, and the ever-present wind lifted her hair from her shoulders with a gentle touch.

"This reminds me of something."

Nick's deep voice rumbled along Jenna's spine, and she had to pull in a deep breath before she turned her head to look at him. He stood in the open doorway to the balcony. Hands in his pockets, he wore black slacks, a gleaming white shirt and a black jacket that looked as if it had been expertly tailored. His dark hair was wind ruffled, his pale eyes were intense, and his jaw was tight.

Her heart tumbled in her chest.

"What's that?" she whispered, amazed that she'd been able to squeeze out a few words.

He stepped out onto the balcony, and with slow, measured steps, walked toward her. "The night we met," he said, taking a place beside her at the railing. "Remember?"

How could she forget? She'd been standing on the Pavilion Deck of *Falcon's Treasure,* the ship she'd been working on at the time. That corner of the ship had been dark and deserted, since most of the passengers preferred spending time in the crowded dance club at the other end of the deck.

So Jenna had claimed that shadowy spot as her own and had gone there nearly every night to stand and watch the sea while the music from the club drifted around her. She'd never run into anyone else there, until the night Nick had stumbled across her.

"I remember," she said, risking a sidelong glance at him. She shouldn't have. He was too close. His eyes too sharp, his mouth too lickable. His scent too rich and too tempting. Her insides twisted and she dropped both hands to the cold, iron railing, holding tight.

"You were dancing, alone in the dark," he said, as if she hadn't spoken at all. As if he were prompting her memory. "You didn't notice me, so I watched you as you swayed to the music, tipping your head back, your hair sliding across your shoulders."

"Nick…"

"You had a smile on your face," he said, his voice

lower now, deeper, and she wouldn't have thought that was possible. "As if you were looking up into the eyes of your lover."

Jenna swallowed hard and shifted uneasily as her body blossomed with heat. With need. "Don't do this, Nick...."

"And I wanted to be the lover you smiled at. The lover you danced with in the dark." He ran the tip of one finger down the length of her arm, and Jenna shivered at the sizzle of something deliciously hot and wicked sliding through her system.

She sucked in a gulp of air, but it didn't help. Her mind was still spinning, her heart racing and her body lighting up like Times Square on New Year's Eve. "Why are you doing this?" she whispered, and heard the desperate plea in her own voice.

"Because I still want you," he said, moving even closer, dropping his hands onto her shoulders and turning her until she was facing him, until their bodies were so close only a single lick of flame separated them. "Because I watched you standing in the moonlight and knew that if I didn't touch you, I'd explode. I want you. Just as I did then. Maybe more."

Oh, she felt the same way. Everything in Jenna clamored at her to move into him. To lean her body against his. To feel the strength and warmth of him surrounding her. But she held back. Determined to fight. To hold on to the reins of the desire that had once steered her down a road that became more rocky the further along she went.

"It would be a mistake," she said, shaking her head, trying to ignore the swell of music, the slide of the trombone, the wail of the saxophone, that seemed to call to something raw and wild inside her. "You know it would."

"No," he said, sliding his hands up, along her shoulders, up the length of her throat, to cup her face between his palms. "This time would be different. This time, we know who we are. This time we know what we're getting into. It's just need, Jenna." His gaze moved over her features, and her breath caught and held in a strangled knot in her chest. "We both feel it. We both want this. Why deny ourselves?"

Why indeed?

Her mind fought with her traitorous body, and Jenna knew that rational thought was going to lose. The need was too great. The desire too hot. The temptation too strong. She did want him. She'd wanted him from the moment she first saw him more than a year ago. She'd missed him, dreamed of him, and now that he was here, touching her, was she really going to turn him down? Walk away? Go to her solitary bed and pray she dreamed of him again?

No.

Was she going to regret this?

Maybe. Eventually.

Was she going to do it?

Oh, yeah.

"There are probably plenty of reasons to deny ourselves," she finally whispered. "But I don't care about any of them." Then she went up on her toes as Nick smiled and flashes of hunger shone in his eyes.

"Atta girl," he murmured and took her mouth in a kiss that stole her breath and set her soul on fire.

His tongue slipped between her lips, stealing into her warmth, awakening feelings that had lain dormant for more than a year. His arms slid around her waist, pulling her in tight. Jenna lifted her own arms and linked them around his neck, holding him to her, silently demanding he deepen the kiss, take more from her.

He did.

His arms tightened until she could hardly draw breath. But who needed air? Jenna groaned, moved into him, pressing her body along his, and she felt the hard length of him jutting against her. That was enough to send even more spirals of heat dancing through her bloodstream.

Again and again, his tongue dipped into her mouth, tasting, exploring, divining her secrets. She gave as well as took, tangling her tongue with his, feeling the molten desire quickening within. He loosened his grip on her and she nearly moaned, but then his hands were moving, up and down her spine, defining every line, every curve. When his palms cupped her bottom and held her to him, she sighed into his mouth and gave herself up to the wonder of his touch.

"I need you," he whispered, dropping his mouth to the line of her jaw, nibbling at her throat.

She turned her head, allowing him easier access, and closed her eyes at the magic of the moment.

Around them, music swelled and the ocean breeze held the two of them in a cool embrace. Moonlight poured down on them from a black, starlit sky, and when Nick lifted his head and looked down at her, Jenna was trapped in his gaze. She read the fire in his eyes, sensed the tautly controlled tension vibrating through his body and felt his need as surely as she did her own.

"Now. Here." He lifted his hands high enough to take hold of the zipper, then slid it down, baring her back to the night wind. Then he pushed the thin straps of her dress down over her shoulders, and Jenna was suddenly glad she hadn't worn a bra beneath that thin, summer fabric.

Now there was nothing separating her from his touch. From the warmth of his hands. He cupped her breasts in his palms and rubbed her tender, aching nipples until she felt the tug and pull right down to the soles of her feet. She swayed into him, letting her head fall back and her eyes close as she concentrated solely on what he was doing to her.

It was everything. His touch, his scent filled her, overwhelming her with a desire that was so much more than she'd once felt for him. In the year since she'd seen him, she'd grown, changed, and now that she was with him again, *she* was more, so she was able to *feel* more.

"Beautiful," he said, his voice no more than a raw scrape of sound. His gaze locked on her breasts, he said, "Even more beautiful than I remembered."

"Nick," she whispered brokenly, "I want—"

"I know," he said, dipping his head, taking first one hardened nipple, then the other into his mouth. His lips and tongue worked that tender flesh, nibbling, licking, suckling, until Jenna's head was spinning and she knew that without his grip on her, she would have fallen into a heap of sensation at his feet.

He pushed her dress the rest of the way down, letting it fall onto the floor, and Jenna was standing in the moonlight, wearing only her high-heeled sandals and her white silk bikini panties. And she felt too covered. Felt as if the fragile lace of her underwear were chafing her skin. All she wanted on her now was Nick. She wanted to lie beneath him, feel his body cover hers, feel him push himself deeply inside her.

She loved him. Heaven help her, she still loved him. Why was it that only Nick could do this to her? Why was he the man her heart yearned for? And what was she going to do about it?

Then he touched her more deeply and those thoughts fled along with any others. All she could do was feel.

"Please," she said on a groan, "please, I need…"

"I need it, too," he told her, lifting her head, looking down into her eyes as he slid one hand down the length of her body, fingertips lightly dusting across her skin. He reached the elastic band of her panties and dipped his hand beneath it to cup her heat.

Jenna rocked into him, leaning hard against him, but Nick didn't let her rest. Instead, he turned her around until her back was pressed to his front and she was facing the wide emptiness of the moonlit sea.

He used one hand to tease and tweak her nipples while the other explored her damp heat. His fingers dipped lower, smoothing across her most tender, sensitive flesh with a feathery caress that only fed the flames threatening to devour her.

Jenna groaned again, lost for words. Her mind had splintered, no thoughts were gathering. She was empty but for the sensations he created. He dipped his head and whispered into her ear, "Watch the sea. See the moonlight. Lose yourself in them while I lose myself in you...."

She did what he asked, fighting to keep her eyes open, and focused on the shimmering sea as he dipped first one finger and then another into her heat. Jenna's breath hitched and she wanted to close her eyes, the better to focus on what he was doing, but she didn't. Instead, she stared unseeing at the broad expanse of sea and sky stretching out into infinity in front of her and fought to breathe as his magic fingers pushed her along a road of sensual pleasure.

He stroked, he delved, he rubbed. His fingers moved over her skin as a concert pianist would touch a grand piano. Her body was his instrument, and she felt his expert's touch with a grateful heart. Again and again, he pushed her, his fingers stroking her from the inside while his thumb tortured one particularly sensitive spot. And while Jenna moaned and twisted in his grasp, her eyes locked on the shimmering sea, she let herself go. She dropped any sense of embarrassment or worry. She pushed aside every stray thought of censure that leaped into her mind, and she devoted herself to the sensory overload she was experiencing.

"Come for me," Nick whispered, his voice no more

than a hush in her ear. His breath dusted her face, her neck, while his fingers continued the gentle, determined invasion. "Let me see you. Let me feel you go over."

His voice was a temptation. Because she was so close to a climax. Her knees trembled. Her body weakened even as it strove to reach the peak Nick was pushing her toward. Her breath came in ragged gasps, her heartbeat thundered in her ears and the tension coiling within was almost more than she could bear. And when she thought she wouldn't survive another moment, she cried out his name and splintered in his arms. Her body shattered, she rode the exquisite wave of completion until she fell at the end only to be caught and held in his strong arms.

Jenna dropped her head onto his shoulder, swallowed hard and fought to speak. "That was—"

"Only the beginning," Nick finished for her and picked her up, swinging her into his arms and stalking back into the suite. He was teetering on the edge of reason. Touching her, feeling her climax roar through her, sensing her surrender, had all come together to build a fire inside him like nothing he'd ever known before.

Seduction had been the plan.

But whose?

He'd thought to use her, feed the need that she'd caused, then be able to let her go. Get her out of his head, out of his blood. But those moments with her on the balcony only made him want more. He had to have her under him, writhing beneath him as he took her.

She lay curled against his chest, in a trusting manner that tore at him even as it touched something inside him he hadn't been aware of. She was trouble. He knew it. Felt it. And couldn't stop himself from wanting.

From having.

In his bedroom Nick strode to the bed, reached down with one hand and grabbed the heavy, black duvet in one fist. Then he tossed it to the foot of the mattress and forgot about it. He laid Jenna down on the white sheets and looked at her for a long moment. The moonlight caressed her here, as well, sliding in through the wide bank of glass that lined his bedroom suite. A silvery glow coated her skin as she stretched like a satisfied cat before smiling up at him.

"Come to me, Nick," she urged, lifting both arms in welcome.

He didn't need a second invitation. Tearing off his clothes, he joined her on the bed, covered her body with his and surrendered to the inevitable. More than a year ago, their first encounter had ended in his bed. Now, it seemed, they'd come full circle.

Nick ran his hands up and down her body and knew he'd never be able to touch her enough. He drew a breath and savored her scent. Dipped his head and tasted her skin at the base of her throat. Her pulse jolted beneath his mouth and he knew she was as eager as he, as needy as he.

He touched her core, delving his fingers into her heat again, and she lifted her hips from the bed, rocking into his hand, moaning and whispering to him.

His body ached and clamored for release. Every inch of him was humming, just touching her. Lying beside her. Jenna. Always Jenna who did this to him. Who turned him into a man possessed, a man who could think of nothing beyond claiming what he knew to be his.

With that thought, Nick tore away from her arms, ignoring the soft sound of disappointment that slipped from her throat. Tugging the drawer on the bedside table open, he reached in, grabbed a condom and, in a few quick seconds, sheathed himself. Then he turned back to her, levering himself over her, positioning himself between her thighs.

He gave her a quick smile. "Last time we forgot that part and look what happened."

"You're right," she said, reaching down to stroke his length, her fingers sliding over the thin layer of latex in a caress that had Nick gulping for air. "Now, will you come to me?"

He spread her thighs farther apart, leaned in close and locked his gaze with hers as his body entered hers. Inch by inch, he invaded her, torturing them both with his deliberately slow thrust.

Her hips moved beneath him, her eyes squeezed shut and she bit her bottom lip. Reaching up, her hands found his upper arms and held on, her short nails digging into his skin, and that was the last straw. The final touch that sent Nick over the edge of reason.

He pushed himself deep inside her and groaned at the tight, hot feel of her body holding his. His hips rocked, setting a rhythm that was both as old as time and new and exciting. She held on tighter, harder, her nails biting into his flesh with a stinging sensation that was counterpoint to the incredible delight of being within her.

Nick moved and she moved with him. Their rhythm set, they danced together, bodies joined, melded, becoming one as they reached for the same, shattering end that awaited them. He stared down into her eyes, losing himself in their depths. She met his gaze and held it until finally, as he felt her body begin to fist around his, she closed her eyes, shrieked his name and shuddered violently as her body exploded from the inside.

His own release came a scant moment later, and Nick heard himself shout as the tremendous relief spilled through him again and again, as if the pleasure would never end.

When he collapsed atop her, he still wasn't sure just who had seduced whom.

Seven

It was a long night.

As if they'd destroyed the invisible barrier keeping them separate, Jenna and Nick came together again and again during the night. Until finally, exhausted, they fell into sleep just before dawn.

When Jenna woke several hours later, she was alone in the big bed. Pushing her hair out of her eyes, she sat up, clutched the silky white sheet to her chest and stared around Nick's room as if half expecting him to appear from the shadows. But he didn't.

Carefully, since her muscles ached, she scooted off the bed, wandered down the hall to her own room and walked directly to the bathroom. As she took a long, hot shower, her mind drifted back to the night before and she wondered if things would be different between them now. But if she thought about that, hoped for it, how much more disappointed would she be if it didn't happen?

Nick had made no promises.

Just as he had made no promises last year during their one amazing week together.

So basically, Jenna told herself, she'd made the same mistake she had before. She'd fallen into bed with a man she loved—despite the fact that he didn't love her.

"Oh, man." She rested her forehead against the aqua and white tiles while the hot, pulsing streams of water pounded against her back. "Jenna, if you're going to make mistakes, and hey, everyone does…at least make *new* ones."

Out of the shower, she dried off and dressed in a pair of white shorts and a dark green tank top. Then she sat on her bed and tried to figure out her next move. The only problem was, she didn't have a clue what to do about what was happening in her world. This had all seemed like such a simple idea. Come to Nick. Tell him about the boys. Go home and slide back into her life.

But now, everything felt…complicated.

Muttering under her breath about stupid decisions and consequences, Jenna glanced at the clock on the bedside table and noticed the phone. Instantly her heart lifted. That's what she needed, she realized. She needed to touch base with the real world. To talk to her sister. To listen to her sons cooing.

Grabbing the receiver, she immediately got the ship's operator, gave them the number she wanted and waited while the phone on the other end of the line rang and rang. Finally, though, Maxie picked up and breathlessly said, "I don't have time for salesmen."

Laughing, Jenna eased back against the headboard of her bed and said, "Hello to you, too."

"Oh, Jenna, it's you." Maxie chuckled a little. "Sorry about that, but your babies are making me a little insane."

She jolted away from the headboard, frowning at the phone in her hand. "Are they okay?"

"*They're* fine," Maxie assured her. "I'm the one who's going to be dead soon. How do you do this every day? If I ever forget to tell you how amazing I think you are, remind me of this moment."

"Thanks, I will. So the boys are good?"

"Happy as clams," her sister said, then paused and idly asked, "although, how do we know clams are happy? It's not like they smile or whistle or something...."

"One of the great mysteries of the universe."

"Amen."

In the background, Jenna heard both the television set blaring and at least one baby crying. "Who is that crying?" she asked.

"Jacob," Maxie told her and her voice was muffled for a minute. "I'm holding Cooper and giving him a bottle and Jake wants his turn. Not exactly rating a ten on the patience scale, that boy."

"True, Jake is a little less easygoing than Cooper." Jenna was quiet then as Maxie brought her up to date on the twins' lives. She smiled as she listened, but her heart ached a little, too. She wanted to be there, holding her sons, soothing them, feeding them. And the fact that she wasn't literally tore at her.

"Bottom line, everything's good here," her sister said finally. "How about you? How did Nick take the news?"

"He doesn't believe me."

"Well, there's a shocker."

Jenna rolled her eyes. Maxie wasn't a big fan of Nick Falco. But then, her sister had been wined, dined and then dumped by a rich guy a couple of years before, and ever since then she didn't have a lot of faith in men in general—and rich men in particular.

"He took the DNA test, though, and was going to have the results faxed to our lab. He should have proof even he can't deny in the next day or two."

"Good. Then you're coming home, right?"

"Yeah." Jenna plucked at the hem of her shorts with her fingertips. She wouldn't stay on board ship for the whole cruise. She'd done what she'd come here to do, and staying around Nick any longer than was necessary was only going to make things even more complicated than they already were.

"I love my nephews," Maxie was saying, "but I think they're as ready to see you as I am."

"I miss them so much." Her heart pinged again as she listened to the angry sound of Jake's cry.

"Uh-huh, now tell me why you really called."

Jenna scowled. "I called to check on my sons."

"Oh, that was part of it. Now let's hear the rest," Maxie said.

"I don't know what you mean."

"Hold on, have to switch babies. Cooper's finished and it's Jake's turn."

Jenna waited and listened to her sister talking to both of the boys, obviously laying Cooper down and picking Jake up as the infant's cries were now louder and more demanding. She smiled to herself when his crying abruptly shut off and knew that he was occupied with his bottle.

"Okay, I'm back," Maxie said a moment later. "Now, tell me what happened between you and Nick."

"What do you mean?"

"You know exactly what I mean and the fact that you're avoiding the question tells me just what happened," her sister said. "You slept with him again, didn't you?"

Jenna's head dropped to the headboard behind her and she stared unseeing up at the ceiling.

"Jenna…"

"There wasn't a lot of sleeping, but yeah."

"Damn it, Jenna—"

She sat up. "I already know it was a mistake, so if you don't mind…"

"A mistake? Forgetting to buy bread at the market is a mistake. Sleeping with a guy who's already dumped you once is a disaster."

"Well, thanks so much," Jenna said drily. "That makes me feel so much better."

Maxie blew out a breath, whispered, "It's okay, Jake, I'm not yelling at you. I'm yelling at your mommy."

Then she said louder, "Fine. Sorry for yelling. But Jenna, you know nothing good can come of this."

"I know." Hadn't she awoken in an empty bed, with no sign of the tender lover she'd spent the night with? Nick couldn't have been more blatant in letting her know just how unimportant she was to him. "God, I know."

"Come home," Maxie urged.

"I will. Soon."

"Now."

"No," Jenna said, shaking her head as she swung her legs off the bed and sat up straight. "I have to talk to him."

"Haven't you said everything there is to say?"

Probably, Jenna thought. After all, it wasn't as if she was going to tell him she loved him. And wasn't that the only piece of information he was missing? Hadn't she done what she'd come here to do? Hadn't she accomplished her mission and more?

"Maxie…"

Her sister blew out a breath, and Jenna could almost see her rolling her eyes.

"I just don't want to see you destroyed again," Maxie finally said. "He's not the guy for you, Jenna, and somewhere deep inside, you know it. You're only asking to get kicked in the teeth again."

The fact that her sister was right didn't change anything. Jenna knew she couldn't leave until she'd seen Nick again. Found out what last night had meant to him, if anything. She had to prove to herself one way or the other that there was no future for them. It was the only way she'd ever be able to let go and make a life for herself and her children.

"If I get hurt again, I'll recover," she said, her voice firming as she continued. "I appreciate you worrying about me, Maxie, but I've got to see this through. So I'll call you when I'm on my way home. Are you sure you're okay to take care of the boys for another couple of days?"

There was a long moment of silence before her sister said, "Yeah. We're fine."

"What about work?" Maxie was a medical transcriber. She worked out of her home, which was a big bonus for those times when Jenna needed a babysitter fast. Like now.

"I work around the babies' nap schedules. I'm keeping up. Don't worry about it."

"Okay, thanks."

"Jenna? Just be careful, okay?"

The door to the suite opened and a maid stepped in. She spotted Jenna, made an apologetic gesture and started to back out again.

"No, wait. It's okay, you can come in now." Then to her sister, she said, "The maid's here, I've got to go. I'll call you soon. And kiss the boys for me, okay?"

When she hung up, Jenna didn't know if she felt better or worse. It was good to know her sons were fine, but Maxie's words kept rattling around in her brain. Yes, her sister was prejudiced against wealthy men, but she had a point, too. Jenna *had* been nearly destroyed after she and Nick had split apart a year ago.

This time, though, she had the distinct feeling that the pain of losing him was going to be much, much worse.

Nick had never thought of himself as a coward.

Hell, he'd fought his way to the top of the financial world. He'd carved out an empire with nothing more than his guts and a dream. He'd created a world that was everything he'd ever wanted.

And yet...a couple of hours ago, he'd slipped out of bed and left Jenna sleeping alone in his room because he hadn't wanted to talk to her.

"Women," he muttered, leaning on the railing at the bow of the Splendor Deck, letting his gaze slide over the shoreline of Acapulco, "always want to *talk* the morning after. Always have to analyze and pick apart everything you'd done and said the night before."

But there was nothing to analyze, he reminded himself. He'd had her, just as he'd planned, and now he was through—also as he'd planned.

Of course his body tightened and his stomach fisted at the thought, but that didn't matter. What mattered was that he'd had Jenna under him, over him, around him, and now he could let her go completely. No more haunted dreams. No more thinking about her at stray moments.

It was finished.

Scowling, he watched as surfers rode the waves into shore while tourists on towels baked themselves to a cherry-red color on the beach. Brightly striped umbrellas were unfurled at intervals along the sand, and waiters dressed in white moved among the crowd delivering tropical drinks.

So if it was finished, why the hell was he still thinking about her?

Because, he silently acknowledged, that night with her had been unlike anything he'd experienced since the last time they'd been together. Nick wasn't a monk. And since he was single, he saw no problem in indulging himself with as many women as he wanted. But no woman had ever gotten to him the way Jenna had.

She made him feel things he had no interest in. Made him want more than he should. That thought both intrigued and bothered him. He wasn't looking for anything more than casual sex with a willing woman. And nothing about Jenna was casual. He already knew that.

So the best thing he could do was stay the hell away from her.

Better for both of them. He pushed away from the railing in disgust. But damned if he'd hide out on his own blasted ship. He'd find Jenna, tell her that he wasn't interested in a replay of last night—and *now* who was lying? Turning, he was in time to see Jenna walking toward him, and everything in him tightened uncomfortably.

In the late-morning sunlight, she looked beautiful. Her blond hair hung loose about her shoulders. Her tank top clung to her breasts—no bra—and his mouth went dry. Her white shorts made her lightly tanned skin look the color of warmed honey. Her dark blue eyes were locked on him, and Nick had to force himself to stand still. To not go to her, pull her up close to him and taste that delectable mouth of hers again.

She hitched her purse a little higher on one bare shoulder and tightened her grip on the strap when she stopped directly in front of him. Whipping her hair back out of her eyes, she looked up at him and said, "I wondered where you disappeared to."

"I had some things to take care of," Nick told her and it was partially true. He'd already fired the band that had refused to clean up their act, hired another one and was expected at a meeting with the harbormaster in a half hour.

But he'd still been avoiding her.

"Look, Nick—"

"Jenna—" he said at the same time, wanting to cut off any attempt by her to romanticize the night before. Bad enough he'd done too much thinking about it already.

"Me first, okay?" she spoke up quickly, before he had a chance to continue. She gave him a half smile, and Nick braced himself for the whole what-do-I-mean-to-you, question-and-answer session. This was why he normally went only for the women who, like him, were looking for nothing more complex than one night of fun. Women like Jenna just weren't on his radar, usually. For good reason.

"I just want to say," she started, then paused for a quick look around to make sure they were alone. They were, since this end of the Splendor Deck was attached to his suite and not accessible to passengers. "Last night was a mistake."

"What?" Not what he'd been expecting.

"We shouldn't have," she said, shaking her head. "Sex with you was not why I came here. It wasn't part of my plan, and right now, I'm really regretting that it happened at all."

Instantly outrage pumped through him. She *regretted* being with him? How the hell was that possible? He'd been there. He'd heard her whimpers, moans and screams. He'd *felt* her surrender. He'd trembled with the force of her climaxes and knew damn well she'd had as good a time as he had. So how the hell could she be regretting it?

More, how could he dump her as per the plan if she was dumping him first?

"Is that right?" he managed to say through gritted teeth.

"Oh, come on, Nick," she said, frowning a bit. "You know as well as I do that it shouldn't have happened. You're only interested in relationships that last the length of a cruise, and I'm a single mom. I'm in no position to be anybody's babe of the month."

"Babe of the month?" He was insulted, and the fact that he'd been about to tell her almost exactly what she was saying to him wasn't lost on him.

She blew out a breath and tightened the already death grip she had on the strap of her purse. "I'm just saying that it won't happen again. I mean, what happened last night. With us. You and me. Not again."

"Yeah, I get it." And now that she'd said that, he wanted her more than ever. Wasn't that a bitch of a thing to admit? Not that he'd give her the satisfaction of knowing what he was thinking. "Probably best that way."

"It is," she said, but her voice sounded a little wistful. Or was he hearing what he wanted to hear?

Strange, a few minutes ago, he'd been thinking of ways to let her go. To tell her they were done. Now that she'd beaten him to the punch, he felt different. What the hell was happening to him, anyway?

Whatever it was, Nick told himself firmly, it was time to nip it in the bud. No way was he going to be tripping on his own heartstrings. Not over a woman he already knew to be an accomplished liar.

Besides, she hadn't come on this trip for him, he told himself sternly, but for what he could give her. She'd booked passage on his ship with the sole purpose of getting money out of him. Sure, it was for child support. But she still wanted money. So what made her different from any other woman he'd known?

"I'm attracted to you," she was saying, and it looked like admitting that was costing her, "but then I guess you already figured that out."

Was she blushing? Did women still do that?

"But I'm not going to let my hormones be in the driver's seat," she told him and met his gaze with a steely determination. "Pretty soon, you'll be back sailing the world with a brunette or a redhead on your arm and I'll be back in Seal Beach taking care of my sons."

The babies.

Hers? His?

He wasn't going there until he knew for sure. Instead,

he decided to turn the tables on her. Remind her just whose ship she was on. Remind her that he hadn't come to her, it had been the other way around.

"Don't get yourself tied up in knots over this, Jenna," he said, reaching out to chuck her under the chin with his fingertips. "It was one night. A blip on the radar screen."

She blinked at him.

"We had a good time," he said lightly, letting none of the tension he felt coiled inside show. "Now it's over. End of story."

He watched as his words slapped at her, and just for a minute he wished he could take them back. Yet as that feeling rushed over him, he wondered where it had come from.

"Okay, then," Jenna said, her voice nearly lost in the rush and swell of the sea below them, tumbling against the ship's hull. "So now we know where we stand."

"We do."

"Well, then," she said, forcing a smile that looked brittle, "maybe I should just fly home early. I can catch a flight out of Acapulco easily enough. I talked to my sister earlier and she's going a little nuts—"

He cut her off instantly. "Are the babies all right?"

She stopped, looked at him quizzically and said slowly, "Yes, of course. The boys are fine, but Maxie's not used to dealing with them twenty-four hours a day and they can be exhausting, so—"

"I'd rather you didn't leave yet," he blurted.

"Why not?"

Because he wasn't ready for her to be gone. But since admitting that even to himself was too lowering, he said, "I want you here until we get the results from the DNA test."

Her gaze dropped briefly, then lifted to meet his again. "You said we'd probably hear sometime today, anyway."

"Then there's no problem with you waiting."

"What's this really about, Nick?" she asked.

"Just what I said," he told her, taking her arm in a firm grip and turning her around. Heat bled up from the spot where his hand rested on her arm. He fought the urge to pull her into him, to dip his head and kiss the pulse beat at the base of her throat. To pull the hem of her shirt up so he could fill his hands with her breasts.

Damn, he was hard and hot and really irritated by that simple fact.

Leading her along the wide walkway, he started for his suite. "We've got unfinished business together, Jenna. And until it's done and over, you're staying."

"Maybe I should get another room."

"Worried you won't be able to control yourself?" he chided as he opened the door and allowed her to precede him into the suite.

"In your dreams," she said shortly, and tossed her purse onto the sofa.

"And yours," he said.

Jenna looked at him and felt herself weakening. It wasn't fair that this was so hard. Wasn't fair that her body wanted and her heart yearned even as her mind told her to back away. She had to leave the ship. Soon.

In the strained silence, a beep sounded from another room, and she glanced at Nick, a question in her eyes.

"Fax machine."

She nodded and as he walked off to get whatever had come in for him, Jenna headed for his bedroom. All she wanted to do was get the underwear she'd left in there the night before. And better to do it while he was occupied somewhere else.

Opening the door, she swung it wide just as Nick called out, "It's from the lab."

If he said anything else, she didn't hear him. Didn't even feel a spurt of pleasure, knowing that now he'd have no choice but to believe her about the fact that he was the father of her sons.

Instead Jenna's gaze was locked on his bed, and her brain short-circuited as she blankly stared at the very surprised, very *naked* redhead stretched out on top of Nick's bed.

Eight

"Jenna?" Nick's voice came from behind her, but she didn't turn.

"Hey!" The redhead's eyes were wide as she scrambled to cover herself—a little too late—with the black duvet. "I didn't know he already had company...."

Nick came up behind Jenna, and she actually felt him tense up. "Who the hell are you?" he demanded, pushing past Jenna to face the woman staring up at him through eyes shining with panic.

"Babe of the month?" Jenna asked curtly.

"Look," the redhead was saying from beneath the safety of the duvet, "I can see I made a mistake here and—"

"Oh," Jenna told her snidely, "don't leave on my

account," then she spun on her heel and marched down the long hall toward her own bedroom.

"Jenna, damn it, wait." Nick's voice was furious but she didn't care. Didn't want to hear his explanation. What could he possibly say? There was a naked woman in his bed. And he hadn't looked surprised, just angry. Which told Jenna everything she needed to know. This happened to him a *lot*.

That simple fact made one thing perfectly clear to Jenna.

It was so past time for her to leave.

God, she was an idiot. To even allow herself to *think* that she loved him. Was she a glutton for punishment?

She marched into her room on autopilot. Blindly she moved to the closet, grabbed her suitcase and tossed it onto the bed. Opening it up, she threw the lid back, then turned for the closet again. Scooping up an armful of her clothes, she carried them to the suitcase, dropped them in and was on her way back to the closet for a second load when Nick arrived.

He stalked right up to her, grabbed her arm and spun her around. "What the hell do you think you're doing?"

She wrenched herself free and gave him a glare that should have fried him on the spot. Jenna was furious and hurt and embarrassed. A dangerous combination. "That should be perfectly obvious, even to you. I'm leaving."

"Because of the redhead?"

"What's the matter, can't remember her name?"

"I've never even *met* her for God's sake," he shouted,

shoving one hand through his hair in obvious irritation, "how the hell should I know her damn name?"

"Stop swearing at me!" Jenna shouted right back. She felt as if every cell in her body was in a stranglehold. Her blood was racing, her mind was in a whirl of conflicting thoughts and emotions, and the only thing she knew for sure was she didn't belong here. Couldn't stay another minute. "I'm leaving and you can't stop me."

"Jenna, damn it, the results from the lab came in—"

Not exactly the way she'd imagined this conversation going, she told herself indignantly. Somehow she'd pictured her and Nick, reading the results together. In her mind, she'd watched as realization came over him. As he acknowledged that he was a father.

Of course, she hadn't pictured a naked redhead being part of the scene.

"Then you know I was telling you the truth. My work here is done." She grabbed up her sneakers, high heels and a pair of flats and tossed them into the suitcase on top of her clothes. Sure it was messy, but she was way past caring.

"We have to talk."

"Oh, we've said all we're going to say to each other," Jenna told him, skipping backward when he made a grab for her again. She didn't trust herself to keep her anger fired if he touched her. "Have your lawyers contact me," she snapped and marched into the connecting bathroom to gather up the toiletries she had scattered across the counter.

"Damn it," Nick said, his voice as tight as the tension coiled inside her. "I just found out I'm a *father,* for God's sake. I need a minute here. If you'll calm down, we can discuss this—"

"Shouldn't you be down the hall with Miss Ready-And-Willing?" Jenna inquired too sweetly as she pushed past him, her things in the crook of her arm.

He shook his head. "She's getting dressed and getting out," he said, grabbing Jenna's arm again to yank her around to face him.

God help her, her body still reacted to his hands on her. Despite everything, she felt the heat, the swell of passion rising inside to mingle with the fury swamping her, and Jenna was sure this wasn't a good thing. She had to get out.

But Nick only tightened his grip. "I didn't invite her. She bribed a maid."

She swallowed hard, lowered her gaze to his hands on her arms and said, "You're hurting me." He wasn't, but her statement was enough to make him release her.

"Jenna—"

"It's a wonder the woman had to bribe anyone. I'm sure the maids are used to letting naked women into your suite. Pretty much a revolving door around here, isn't it?"

"Nobody gets into my suite unless I approve it, which I didn't in this case," Nick added quickly. "And I hope for the maid's sake that it was a *good* bribe, because it just cost her her job."

"Oh, that's nice," Jenna said as she turned to zip her

suitcase closed. "Fire a maid because you're the horniest male on the face of the planet."

"Excuse me?"

Jenna straightened up, folded her arms across her chest and tapped the toe of her sandal against the floor as she glared up at him. "Everyone on this ship knows what a player you are, Nick. Probably wasn't a big surprise to the maid that a woman wanted into your suite and for all she knew, you *did* want her here."

He glared right back at her. "My life is my business."

"You're right it is." She grabbed the handle of her suitcase and slid it off the bed. Jenna didn't even care if she'd left something behind. She couldn't stay here a second longer. She had to get away from Nick, off this ship and back to the world that made sense. The world where she was wanted. Needed.

"And I don't owe you an explanation for anything," he pointed out unnecessarily.

"No, you don't. Just as you don't have to fire a maid because she assumed it was business as usual around here." Jenna shook her head, looked him up and down, then fixed her gaze on his. "But you do what you want to, Nick. You always do. Blame the maid. Someone who works hard for a living. Fire her. Make yourself feel better. Just don't expect me to hang around to watch."

"Damn it, Jenna, I'm not letting you walk out." He moved in closer and she felt the heat of his body reaching out for her. "I want to know about my sons. I want to talk about what we're going to do now."

Tightening her grip on the suitcase handle, Jenna

swung her hair back behind her shoulders and said softly, "What we're going to do now is go back to our lives. Contact your lawyer, set up child support. I'll send you pictures of the boys. I'll keep you informed of what's happening with them."

"It's not enough," he muttered, his voice low and deep and hard.

"It'll have to be, because it's all I can give you." Jenna walked past him, headed for the living room and the purse she'd left on a sofa. But she stopped in the doorway and turned for one last look at him.

Diffused sunlight speared through the bank of windows and made his dark hair shine. His eyes were shadowed and filled with emotions she couldn't read, and his tall, leanly muscled body was taut with a fury that was nearly tangible.

Everything in her ached for him.

But she'd just have to learn to live with disappointment. "Goodbye, Nick."

Jenna was gone.

So was the redhead.

And he didn't fire the maid.

Nick hated like hell that Jenna had been right about that, but how could he fire some woman when everyone on the damn ship knew he had women coming and going all the time? Instead, he'd had Teresa demote the maid to the lower decks and instructed her to make it clear that if the woman ever took another bribe from a guest, she'd be out on her ass.

Sitting at the desk in his office, he turned his chair so that he faced the sprawl of the sea. He wasn't seeing the last of the day's sunlight splashing on the water like fistfuls of diamonds spread across its surface. He didn't notice the wash of brilliant reds and violets as sunset painted a mural across the sky. Instead his mind continued to present him with that last look he'd had of Jenna. Standing in the open doorway of her bedroom, suitcase in her hand, wearing an expression that was a combination of regret and disappointment.

"What right does she have to be disappointed in me? And why the hell do I care what she thinks?" he muttered. He'd meant to have her and let her go. It had been a good plan and that's exactly what had happened. He ought to be pleased. Instead, his brain continued to ask him just why Jenna had been so pissed about the redhead.

Was she being territorial?

Did she really care for him?

Did it matter?

Then he glanced down at the single sheet of paper he still held in his hand. The fax from the lab in San Pedro was clear and easy to read.

His DNA matched that of Jenna's twins.

Nick Falco was a father.

He was both proud and horrified.

"I have two sons," he said, needing to hear the words said aloud. He shook his head at the wonder of it and felt something in his chest squeeze tightly until it was almost impossible to draw a breath.

He was a *father.*

He had *family.*

Two tiny boys who weren't even aware of his existence were only alive because of *him.* Pushing up from his chair, he walked to the wide bank of glass separating him from the ocean beyond and leaned one hand on the cool surface of the window. Sons. Twins. He felt that twist of suppressed emotion again and murmured, "The question is, how do I handle it? What's the best way to manage this situation?"

Jenna had left, assuming that he'd keep his distance. Deal with her through the comforting buffer of an attorney. He scowled at the sea and felt a small but undeniable surge of anger begin to rise within him, twisting with that sense of pride and confusion until he nearly shook with the rush of emotions he wasn't used to experiencing.

He was a man who deliberately kept himself at a distance from most people. He liked having that comfort zone that prevented anyone from getting too close. Now, though, that was going to change. It had to change.

Jenna thought she knew him. Thought he'd be content to remain a stranger to his sons. Thought he'd go on with his life, putting her and Jacob and Cooper aside. Knowing her, she thought he'd be satisfied to be nothing more than a fat wallet to his sons.

"She's wrong," he muttered thickly, and his hand on the glass fisted. "I may not know anything about being a father, but those boys are *mine.* And I'll be damned if I let *anyone* keep me from them."

Turning around, he hit a button on the intercom and ground out, "Teresa?"

"Yes, boss?"

He folded the DNA report, tucked it into the breast pocket of his shirt and said, "Call the airport. Hire a private jet. I'm going back to California."

By the following morning, it was almost as if Jenna had never been gone. She'd stopped on the way home from the airport the night before to pick up the boys at Maxie's house. She hadn't been able to bear the thought of being away from them another minute. With the twins safely in their rooms and her suitcase unpacked, Jenna was almost able to convince herself that she'd never left. That the short-lived cruise hadn't happened. That she hadn't slept with Nick again. That she hadn't left him with a naked redhead in his bedroom.

The pain of that slid down deep inside, where she carefully buried it. After all, none of that had anything to do with reality. The cruise—Nick—had been a short jaunt to the other side of the fence. Now she was back where she belonged.

She'd been awake for hours already. The twins didn't take into consideration the fact that Mom hadn't gotten much sleep last night. They still wanted breakfast at six o'clock in the morning. Now she was sitting on the floor in the middle of her small living room, working while she watched her boys.

"I missed you guys," she said, looking over at her sons as they each sat in a little jumper seat. The slightest motion they made had the seat moving and shaking, which delighted them and brought on bright, toothless grins.

Jake waved one fist and bounced impatiently while Cooper stared at his mother as if half-afraid to take his eyes off her again for fear she might disappear.

"Your aunt Maxie said you were good boys," she said, talking to them as she always did. Folding the first load of laundry for the day, Jenna paused to inhale the soft, clean scent of their pajamas before stacking them one on top of the other. "So because I missed you so much and you were so good, how about we walk to the park this afternoon?"

This was what Jenna wanted out of her life, she thought. Routine. Her kids. Her small but cozy house. A world that was filled with, if not excitement, then lots of love. And if her heart hurt a little because Nick wasn't there and would never know what it was to be a part of his sons' lives, well, she figured she'd get over it. Eventually. Shouldn't take more than twenty or thirty years.

The doorbell had her looking up, frowning. Then she glanced at the twins. "You weren't expecting anyone, were you?"

Naturally, she didn't get an answer, so she grinned, pushed herself to her feet and stepped around them as she walked the short distance to her front door. Glancing over her shoulder, she gave the living room a quick look to make sure everything was in order.

The couch was old but comfortable, the two arm

chairs were flowered, with bright throw pillows tucked into their corners. The tables were small, and the rag rug on the scarred but polished wooden floors were handmade by her grandmother. Her home was just as she liked it. Cozy. Welcoming.

She was still smiling when she opened the front door to find Nick standing there. His dark hair was ruffled by the wind, his jeans were worn and faded, and the long-sleeved white shirt he wore tucked into those jeans was open at the throat. He looked way too good for her self-control. So she shifted her gaze briefly to the black SUV parked at the curb in front of her house. That explained *how* he'd gotten there. Now the only thing to figure out was *why* he was there.

Looking back up into his face, she watched as he pulled off his dark glasses, tucked an arm into the vee of his shirt and looked into her eyes. "Morning, Jenna."

Morning? "What?"

"Good to see you, too," he said, giving her a nod as he stepped past her into the house.

"Hey! You can't just—" Her gaze swept over him and landed on the black duffle bag he was carrying. "What are you doing here? Why're you here? How did you find me?"

He stopped just inside the living room, dropped his duffel bag to the floor and shoved both hands into the back pockets of his jeans. "I came to see my sons," he said tightly. "And trust me when I say it wasn't hard to find you."

"Nick…"

"And I brought you this." He pulled a small, sealed envelope out of his back pocket and handed it over. "It's from your friend Mary Curran. She was upset when she found out that you'd left the ship."

Jenna winced. She hadn't even thought of saying goodbye to the friend she'd made, and a twinge of guilt tugged at her.

"She said this is her telephone number and her e-mail address." He stared at her. "She wants you to keep in touch."

"I, uh, thanks." She took the envelope.

He looked at her, hard and cold. His pale eyes were icy and his jaw was clenched so tightly it was a wonder his teeth weren't powder. "Where are they?" he demanded.

Her mouth snapped closed, but she shot a look at the boys, jiggling in their bouncy seats. Nick followed her gaze and slowly turned. She watched as the expression on his face shifted, going from cool disinterest to uncertainty. Jenna couldn't remember ever seeing Nick Falco anything less than supremely confident.

Yet it appeared that meeting his children for the first time was enough to shake even his equilibrium.

Walking toward them slowly, he approached the twins as he would have a live grenade. Jenna held her breath as she watched him gingerly drop to his knees in front of the bouncy seats and let his gaze move from one baby boy to the other. His eyes held a world of emotions that she'd never thought to see. Usually he guarded what he was thinking as diligently as a pit bull on a short chain. But now…Jenna's heart ached a little in reaction to Nick's response to the babies.

"Which one is which?" he whispered, as if he didn't completely trust his voice.

"Um—" She walked a little closer, her sneakers squeaking a bit as she stepped off the rug onto the floor.

"No, wait," he said, never looking at her, never taking his gaze off the twins, "let me." Tentatively, Nick reached out one hand and gently cupped Jacob's face in his big palm. "This one's Jake, right?"

"Yes," she said, coming up beside him, looking down at the faces of her sons who were both looking at Nick in fascination. As usual, though, Jacob's mouth was open in a grin and Cooper had tipped his little head to one side as if he really needed to study the situation a bit longer before deciding how he felt about it.

"So then, you're Cooper," Nick said and with his free hand, stroked that baby's rounded cheek.

Jenna's breath hitched in her chest and tears gathered in her eyes. God, over the past several months, she'd imagined telling Nick about the boys, but she'd never allowed herself to think about him actually meeting them.

She'd never for a moment thought that he would be interested in seeing them. And now, watching his gentle care with her boys made her heart weep and every gentle emotion inside her come rushing to the surface. There was just something so tender, so poignant about this moment, that Jenna's throat felt too tight to let air pass. When she thought she could speak again without hearing her voice break, she said, "You really were listening when I told you about them."

"Of course," he acknowledged, still not looking at her, still not tearing his gaze from the two tiny boys who had him so enthralled. "They're just as you described them. They look so much alike, and yet, their personalities are so obvious when you're looking for the differences. And you were right about something else, too. They're beautiful."

"Yeah, they are," she said, her heart warming as it always did when someone complimented her children. "Nick," she asked a moment later, because this was definitely something she needed to know, "why have you come here?"

He stood up, faced her, then glanced again at his sons, a bemused expression on his face. "To see them. To talk to you. After you left, I did a lot of thinking. I was angry at you for leaving."

"I know. But I had to go."

He didn't address that. Instead he said, "I came here to tell you I'd come up with a plan for dealing with this situation. A way for each of us to win."

"Win?" she repeated. "What do you mean 'win'?"

Shifting his pale blue gaze back to hers, his features tightened, his mouth firming into a straight, grim line. A small thread of worry began to unspool inside of her, and Jenna had to fight to keep from grabbing up her kids and clutching them to her chest.

Only a moment ago she'd been touched by Nick's

first sight of his sons. Now the look on his face told her she wasn't going to be happy with his "plan."

"Look," he said, shaking his head, sparing another quick glance for the babies watching them through wide, interested eyes, "it came to me last night that there was an easy solution to all of this."

"I didn't come to you needing a solution. All I wanted from you is child support."

"Yeah, well, you'll get that." He waved one hand as if brushing aside something that didn't really matter. "But I want more."

That thread of worry thickened and became a ribbon that kept unwinding, spreading a dark chill through her bloodstream that nearly had her shivering as she asked, "How much more?"

"I'm getting to that," he said. "Like I said, I've been doing a lot of thinking since you left the ship. And finally, last night on the flight up here, it occurred to me that twins are a lot of work for any one parent."

What was he getting at? Why was he suddenly shifting his gaze from hers, avoiding looking at her directly? And why had she ever gone to him? "Yes, it is, but—"

"So my plan was simple," he said, interrupting her before she could really get going. "We split them up, each of us taking one of the twins."

"What?"

Nine

Nick couldn't blame her for the outrage.

She jumped in front of the babies and held her arms up and extended as if to fight him off should he try to grab the twins and run. "Are you insane? You can't split them up," she said, keeping her voice low and hard. "They aren't *puppies*. You don't get the pick of the litter. They're little boys, Nick. Twins. They need each other. They need *me*. And you can't take either of them away from me."

He'd already come to the same conclusion. All it had taken was one look at the boys, sitting in their little seats, so close that they could reach out and touch each other. But he hadn't known until he'd seen them.

"Relax," he said, lifting one hand to try to stop her

from taking off on another rant. "I said that's the plan I *did* have. Things have changed."

"You've been here ten seconds. What could have changed?" She was still defensive, standing in front of her sons like a knight of old. All she really needed was a battle-ax in her hands to complete the picture.

"I saw them," he said, and something in his voice must have reached her because her shoulders eased down from their rigid stance. "They're a unit. We can't split them up. I get that."

"Good." She blew out a breath. "That's good."

"I'm not finished," he told her, and watched as her back snapped straight as a board again. "I came here to see my sons, and now that I have, I'm not going anywhere."

She looked stunned, her mouth dropping open, her big, blue eyes going even wider than usual. "What do you mean?" Then, as she began to understand exactly what he meant, she shook her head fiercely. "You can't possibly think you're going to stay here."

This was turning out to be more fun than he'd thought it would be.

"Yeah, I am." Nick glanced around the small living room. You could have dropped two entire houses the size of hers into his suite on the ship, and yet there was something here that was lacking in his place, despite the luxury. Here, he told himself, she'd made a home. For her and their sons. A home he had no intention of leaving. At least not for a while. Not until he'd gotten to know his sons. Not until he'd come up with a way that he could be a part of their lives.

"That's crazy."

"Not at all," he said tightly, his gaze boring into hers. "They're my sons. I've already lost four months of their lives and I'm not going to lose any more."

"But Nick—"

He interrupted her quickly. "I won't be just a check to them, Jenna. And if that's what you were hoping for, sorry to disappoint."

She chewed at her bottom lip, folded her arms over her chest as if she were trying to hold herself together and finally said, "You can't stay here. There's no room. It's a two-bedroom cottage, Nick. One for the boys, one for me and you're *not* staying in my room, I guarantee that."

His body tightened and he thought he just might be able to change her mind on that front, eventually. But for now, "I'll bunk on the couch."

"But—"

"Look," Nick said. "It's simple. I stay here, get to know my kids. Or," he added, pulling out the big guns, "I sue you for sole custody. And which one of us do you think would win that battle? Your choice, Jenna. Which will it be?"

Her face paled, and just for a second Nick felt like a complete bastard. Then he remembered that he was fighting for the only family he had. His sons. And damned if he'd lose. Damned if he'd feel guilty for wanting to be a part of their lives however he had to manage it.

"You would do that?"

"In a heartbeat."

"You really are a callous jerk, aren't you?"

"I am whatever I have to be to get the job done," Nick told her.

"Congratulations, then. You win this round."

One of the babies began to cry, as if sensing the sudden tension in the room. Nick glanced down to see that it was Jacob, his tiny face scrunched up as fat tears ran down his little cheeks. An instant later, taking his cue from his brother, Cooper, too, let out a wail that was both heart wrenching and terrifying to Nick.

He threw a panicked look at Jenna, who only shook her head.

"You want a crash course in fatherhood, Nick?" She waved a hand at the boys, whose cries had now reached an ear-splitting range as they thrashed and kicked and waved their little arms furiously. "Here's lesson one. You made them cry. Now you make them stop."

"Jenna—"

Then, while he watched her dumbfounded, she scooped up the stack of freshly folded baby clothes and walked off down a short hallway to disappear into what he guessed was the boys' bedroom, leaving him alone with his frantic sons.

"Great," Nick muttered as he dropped to his knees in front of the twins. "This is just going great. Good job, Nick. Way to go."

As he dropped to his knees, jiggled the bouncy seats and pleaded with the boys to be quiet, he had the distinct feeling he was being watched. But if Jenna was standing in the shadows observing his performance, he didn't really want to know. So he concentrated on his sons and told himself that a man who could build a cruise ship line out of nothing should be able to soothe a couple of crying babies.

After all, how hard could it be?

By the end of the afternoon, Nick was on the ragged edge and Jenna was enjoying the show. He'd fed the boys, bathed them—which was entertainment enough that she wished she'd videotaped the whole thing—and now as he was trying to get them dressed. Jenna stood in the doorway to the nursery, silently watching with a delighted smile on her face.

"Come on, Cooper," Nick pleaded. "Just let me get this shirt on and then we'll—" He stopped, sniffed the air, then turned a horrified look on Jacob. "Did you?" He sniffed again. "You did, didn't you? And I just put that diaper on you."

Jenna slapped one hand over her mouth and watched Nick in a splash of sunlight slanting through the opened louvred blinds. The walls were a pale green and boasted a mural she'd painted herself while pregnant. There were trees and flowers and bunnies and puppies, painted in bright, primary colors, racing through the garden. A white dresser stood at one end of the room and an over-stuffed rocking chair was tucked into a corner.

And now there was Nick.

Staring down into the crib where he'd laid both boys for convenience sake, Nick shoved both hands through his hair—something he'd been doing a lot—and muttered something she didn't quite catch.

Still, she didn't offer to help.

He hadn't asked for any, and Jenna thought it was only fair that he get a real idea of what her days were like. If nothing else, it should convince him that he was *so* not ready to be a single parent to twin boys.

"Okay, Coop," he said with a tired sigh, "I'll get your shirt on in a minute. First, though, I've got to do something about your brother before we all asphyxiate."

Jenna chuckled, and Nick gave her a quick look. "Enjoying this, are you?"

"Is that wrong?" she asked, still grinning.

He scowled at her, then shook his head and wrinkled his nose. "Fine, fine. Big joke. But you have to admit, I'm not doing badly."

"I suppose," she conceded with a nod. "But smells to me as if you've got a little problem facing you at the moment."

"And I'll handle it," he said firmly, as though he was trying to convince himself, as well as her.

"Okay then, get to it."

He scrubbed one hand across his face, looked down into the crib and murmured, "How can someone so cute smell so bad?"

"Yet another universal mystery," she told him.

"Another?"

"Never mind," Jenna said, thinking back to her conversation with Maxie when Jenna was still on the ship. Before the redhead. Before she'd left in such a hurry.

Oh God. Jenna straightened up and closed her eyes. Maxie. Wait until *she* found out that Nick was here.

"You okay?" he asked.

Opening her eyes again, she looked at him, so out of place there in her sons' nursery, and told herself that this was just what he'd said their night together was. Nothing more than a blip on the radar. One small step outside the ordinary world. Once he'd made his point, got to know his sons a little, he'd be gone again and everything would go back to the way it was supposed to be.

Which was good, right?

"Jenna?"

"Huh? Oh. Yeah. I'm fine. Just…thinking."

He looked at her for a long second or two as if trying to figure out just what she'd been thinking. Thankfully, mind reading was *not* one of his skills.

"Right."

"So," Jenna said softly, "are you going to take care of Jake's little problem or do you need a rescue?"

He didn't look happy, but he also didn't look like he was going to beg off.

"No, I don't need a rescue. I said I could take care of them and I can." He took a breath, frowned again and reached into the crib.

Jenna heard the tear of the Velcro straps on the disposable diaper, then heard Nick groan out, "Oh my God."

Laughing, she turned around and left him to his sons.

Though it made her crazy, Jenna spent the rest of the day in her small garage, working on a gift basket that was to be delivered in two days. If Nick wanted to play at being a father, then she'd just let him see what it was like dealing with twin boys.

It felt strange to be right there at the house and still be so separate from the boys, but she had to make Nick see that he was in no way prepared to be a father. Had to make him see that taking her sons away from her would be a bad idea all the way around.

Just thinking about his threat sent cold chills up and down her spine, though. He was rich. He could afford the best lawyers in the country. He could hire nannies and bodyguards and buy whatever the court might think the boys would need.

"And where does that leave me?"

A single mom with a pitifully small bank account and an office in her garage. She'd have no chance at all if Nick really decided to fight her for their sons.

But why would he? That thought kept circling in her mind and she couldn't shake it. Was this all to punish her? Was it nothing more than a show of force? But why would he go to such lengths?

Shaking her head, she wrapped the completed basket with shrink-wrap cellophane, plugged in her travel-size hair dryer and focused the hot air on the clear plastic wrap. As she tucked and straightened and pulled, the gift basket began to take shape, and she smiled to herself despite the frantic racing in her mind.

When she was finished, she left the basket on her worktable where, in the morning, she'd affix a huge red bow to the top before packing it up to be delivered. For now, though, she was tired, hungry and very curious to see how Nick was doing with the boys.

She slipped into the kitchen through the connecting door and stopped for an appalled moment as she let her gaze sweep the small and usually tidy room. The red walls and white cabinets were pretty much all she recognized. There was spilled powdered formula strewn across the round tabletop, discarded bottles that hadn't been rinsed and a *tower* of dirty receiving blankets that Nick had apparently used to wipe up messes.

Shaking her head, she quietly walked into the living room, half-afraid of what she would find. There wasn't a sound in the house. No TV. No crying babies. Nothing.

Frowning, she moved farther into the room, noticing more empty baby bottles, and a torn bag of diapers spilled across a tabletop next to an open and drying-out box of baby wipes. Then she rounded the sofa and stopped dead. Nick was stretched out, fast asleep on her grandmother's rag rug and on either side of him lay a sleeping baby.

"Oh, my." Jenna simply stood there, transfixed by the sight of Nick and their sons taking a nap together. A single lamp threw a puddle of golden light across the three of them even as the last of the sunlight came through the front window. Nick's even breathing and the soft sighs and coos issuing from the twins were the only sounds in the room and Jenna etched this image into her mind so that years from now she could call up this mental picture and relive the moment.

There was just something so sweet, so *right* about the little scene. Nick and his sons. Together at last.

Her heart twisted painfully in her chest as love for all three of them swamped her. Oh, she was in so much trouble. Loving Nick was not a smart thing to do. She knew there was no future there for them. All he wanted was to be a part of her sons' lives—that didn't include getting close with their mother. So, what was she supposed to do? How could she love Nick when she knew that nothing good could come of it? And how could she keep her sons from him when she knew, deep down, that they would need a father as much as Nick would need them?

"Why does it have to be you who touches my heart?" she whispered, looking down at the man who'd invaded her life and changed her world.

And as she watched him, Nick's eyes slowly opened and his steady stare locked on her. "Do I?" he asked quietly.

Caught, there was no point in trying to deny what she'd already admitted aloud. She dropped to her knees. "You know you do."

Carefully, so as not to disturb the twins, Nick sat up, wincing a little at the stiffness in his back. But his gaze didn't waver. He continued to meet her eyes, and Jenna wished she could read what he was thinking. What he was feeling.

But as always, Nick's thoughts were his own, his emotions so completely controlled she didn't have a clue what was going on behind those pale blue eyes.

"Then why'd you leave the ship so fast?" Nick asked quietly.

"You know why." Just the memory of the naked redhead was enough to put a little steel back into her spine.

"I didn't even know her," he reminded her with just a touch of defensiveness in his voice.

"Doesn't matter," she said, lowering her voice quickly when Jacob began to stir. She hadn't meant to wake him up. Hadn't wanted to get into any of this right now. But since it had happened anyway, there was no point in trying to avoid it. "Nick, don't you see? The redhead was just a shining example of how different we are. She brought home to me how much out of my element I was on that ship. With you."

He reached out, skimmed his fingertips along her cheek and pushed her hair back behind her right ear. Jenna shivered at the contact, but took a breath and steadied herself. Want wasn't enough. A one-sided love wasn't enough. She needed more. Deserved more.

"I don't belong in the kind of life you lead, Nick. And neither do the boys."

"You could, though," he told her, his voice a hush of sound that seemed intimate, cajoling. "All three of you could. We could all live on the ship. You know there's plenty of room. The boys would have space to play. They'd see the world. Learn about different cultures, different languages."

Tempting, so tempting, just as he'd meant it to be. A reluctant smile curved her mouth, but she shook her head as she looked from him to the twins and back again. "They can't have a real life living on board a ship, Nick. They need a backyard. Parks. School. Friends—" She stopped, waved both hands and added, "A *dog*."

He tore his gaze from hers and looked at first one sleeping baby to the other before shifting his gaze back to hers. "We'll hire tutors. They can play with the passengers' kids. We could even have a dog if they want one. It could work, Jenna. We could make it work."

Though a part of her longed to believe him, she knew, deep down, that this wasn't about him wanting to be with her—finding a way to integrate her into his life—this was about him discovering his sons and wanting them with him.

"No, Nick," she whispered, shaking her head sadly. "It wouldn't be fair to them. Or us. You don't want me, you want your sons. And I understand that. Believe me I do."

He grabbed for her hand and smoothed the pad of his thumb across her knuckles. "It's not just the boys, Jenna. You and I…"

"Would never work out," she finished for him, despite the flash of heat sweeping from her hand, up her arm, to rocket around her chest like a pinball slapping against the tilt bar.

She wished it were different. Wished it were possible that he could love her as she did him. But Nick Falco simply wasn't the kind of man to commit to any one woman. Best that she remember that and keep her heart as safe as she could.

"You don't know that. We could try." His eyes were so filled with light, with hunger and the promise of something delicious that made Jenna wish with everything in her that she could take the risk.

But it wasn't only herself she had to worry about now. There were two other little hearts it was her job to protect. And she couldn't bring herself to take a chance that might bring her sons pain a few years down the road.

But instead of saying any of that, instead of arguing the point with him, she pulled her hand free of Nick's grasp and said softly, "Help me get the boys up to bed, okay?"

He drew up one leg and braced one arm across his knee. His gaze was locked on her, his features half in shadow, half in light. "This isn't over, Jenna."

As she bent over to scoop up Jacob, Jenna paused, looked into those pale blue eyes and said, "It has to be, Nick."

Ten

"Here?" Maxie repeated. "What do you mean he's here? Here in Seal Beach here?"

Jenna glanced back over her shoulder at her closed front door. She'd spotted Maxie pulling up out front and had made a beeline for the door to head her off at the pass, so to speak. "I mean he's *here* here. In the house here. With the boys here."

For three days now. She'd been able to avoid Maxie by putting her off with phone calls, claiming to be busy. But Jenna had known that sooner or later, her older sister would just drop by.

"Are you *nuts?*" Maxie asked. Her big, blue eyes went wide as saucers and her short, spiky, dark blond hair actually looked spikier somehow, as if it were actually standing on end more than usual. "What are you thinking, Jenna? Why would you invite him here?"

"I didn't invite him," Jenna argued, then shrugged. "He...came."

Maxie stopped, narrowed her eyes on Jenna and asked, "Are you sleeping with him?"

Disappointment and need tangled up together in the center of Jenna's chest. No, she wasn't sleeping with him, but she was dreaming of him every night, experiencing erotic mental imagery like she'd never known before. She was waking up every morning with her body aching and her soul empty.

But she was guessing her older sister didn't want to hear that, either, so instead, she just answered the question.

"No, Saint Maxie, defender of all morals," Jenna snapped, "I'm *not* sleeping with him. He's been on the couch the last couple of nights and—"

"Couple of nights?"

Jenna winced, then looked up and waved at her neighbor, who'd stopped dead-heading her roses to stare at Maxie in surprise. "Morning, Mrs. Logan."

The older woman nodded and went back to her gardening. Jenna shifted her gaze up and down the narrow street filled with forties-era bungalows. Trees lined the street, spreading thick shade across neatly cropped lawns. From down the street came the sound of a basketball being bounced, a dog barking maniacally and the muffled whir of skateboard wheels on asphalt. Just another summer day. And Jenna wondered just how many of her neighbors were enjoying Maxie's little rant. Shooting her sister a dark look, Jenna lifted both eyebrows and waited.

Maxie took the hint and lowered her voice. "Sorry, sorry. But I can't believe Nick Falco's been here for two nights and you didn't tell me."

Jenna smirked at her. "Gee, me, neither. Of course, I only kept it a secret because I thought you might not understand, but clearly I was wrong."

"Funny."

Jenna blew out a breath and hooked her arm through her sister's. No matter what else was going on in her life, Maxie and she were a team. They'd had only each other for the last five years, after their parents were killed in a car accident. And she wasn't going to lose her only sister in an argument over a man who didn't even *want* her.

"Max," she said, trying to keep her voice even and calm, despite the whirlwind of emotions she felt churning inside, "he's here to get to know the boys. His sons, remember? We're not together that way, and believe me when I say I'm being careful."

Maxie didn't look convinced, but then she wasn't exactly a trusting soul when it came to men. Not that Jenna could blame her or anything…not after she was so unceremoniously dumped by that jerk Darius Stone.

"This is a bad idea," Maxie said, as if she hadn't already made herself perfectly clear.

"He won't be here long."

"His kind don't need much time."

"Maxie…"

"You sure he's not staying?"

"Why would he?"

"I can think of at least three reasons off the top of my head," she countered. "Jacob, Cooper and oh, yeah, *you*. So I ask it again. Are you sure he's not staying for long?"

Hmm. No, she wasn't. In fact, Jenna would have thought that Nick would have had his baby fix by now and be all too glad to go back to his life. But so far he hadn't shown any signs of leaving.

Was it just the boys keeping him here?

Or did he feel something for her, too?

Oh God, she couldn't allow herself to start thinking that way. It was just setting herself up for more damage once he really did leave.

"Jenna—" Nick called to her from the front porch, then stopped when he saw Maxie and her talking and added, "Oh. Sorry."

No way to avoid this, Jenna thought dismally, already regretting putting her sister and her ex-lover in the same room together. But she forced a smile anyway. "It's okay, Nick. This is my sister, Maxie."

When neither of them spoke, Jenna gave Max a nudge with her elbow.

"Fine, fine," Max muttered, then raised her voice and said grudgingly, "Nice to meet you."

"Yeah. You, too."

"Well, isn't this special?" Jenna murmured, and wondered if she could get frostbite from the chill in the air between these two. "Come on in, Max," she urged, wanting her sister to see that she had nothing to worry about. That Nick wasn't interested in her and that she wasn't going to be pining away when he left. Surely, Jenna thought, she was a good enough actor to pull that off. "See the boys. Have some coffee."

Still looking at Nick, Maxie shook her head and said, "I don't know…"

"I went out for doughnuts earlier," Nick offered.

"Is he trying to bribe me?" Maxie whispered.

Jenna snorted a laugh. "For God's sake, Max, be nice." But as she followed her sister into the house, Jenna could only think that this must have been what it felt like to be dropped behind enemy lines with nothing more than a pocketknife.

Nick knew he should have left already.

Then he wouldn't have had to deal with Jenna's sister. Although, she'd finally come around enough that she hadn't looked as if she wanted to stab him to death with the spoon she used to stir her coffee.

The point was, though, with access to a private jet, he could catch up with the ship in Fort Lauderdale in time to enjoy the second half of the cruise to Italy. Then he wouldn't have to play nice with Jenna's sister—who clearly hated his guts. And he wouldn't be tormented by the desire he felt every waking moment around Jenna herself.

The last couple of nights he'd spent on her lumpy couch had been the longest of his life. He lay awake late into the night, imagining striding down the short hall to her bedroom, slipping into her bed and burying himself inside her. He woke up every morning so tight and hard he felt as if he might explode with the want and frustration riding him. And seeing her first thing in the morning, smelling the floral scent of her shampoo, watching her sigh over that first sip of coffee was another kind of torture.

She was here.

But she wasn't his.

Now Jenna was off to a packaging store, mailing out one of her gift baskets, and he was alone with his sons.

Nick walked into the boys' nursery to find them both wide awake, staring up at the mobiles hanging over their beds. The one over Jake's crib was made up of brightly colored animals, dancing now in the soft breeze coming in from the partially opened window. And over Cooper's bed hung a mobile made up of bright stars and smiling crescent moons.

He looked from one boy to the other, noting their similarities and their differences. Each of them had soft, wispy dark hair and each of them had a dimple—just like Nick's—in their left cheek. Both boys had pale blue eyes, though Cooper's were a little darker than his brother's.

And both of them had their tiny fists wrapped around his heart.

"How am I supposed to leave you?" he asked quietly. "How can I go back to my life, not knowing what you're doing? Not knowing if you've gotten a tooth or if you've started crawling. How can I not be here when you start to walk? Or when you fall down for the first time?"

Soft sunlight came through the louvered blinds on the

window and lay across the shining wood floor like gold bars. Outside somewhere on this cozy little street, a lawn-mower fired up and Jake jumped as though he'd been shot.

Instantly Nick moved to the crib, leaned over and laid one hand on his son's narrow chest. He felt the rapid-fire thud of a tiny heart beneath his palm, and a love so deep, so pure, so all encompassing, filled him to the point that he couldn't draw a breath.

He hadn't expected this. Hadn't thought to fall so helplessly in love with children he hadn't known existed two weeks ago. Hadn't thought that he'd enjoy getting up at the crack of dawn just so he could look down into wide eyes, eager to explore the morning. Hadn't thought that being here, with the boys, with their mother, could feel so…right.

Now that he knew the truth, though, the question was, what was he going to do about it?

Moving across the room to Cooper, he bent down, scooped his son up into his arms and cradled him against his chest. The warm, pliant weight of him and his thoughtful expression made Nick smile. He drew the tip of one finger along Cooper's cheek, and the infant boy turned his face into that now-familiar touch. Nick's heart twisted painfully in his chest as he stared down into those solemn blue eyes so much like his own.

"I promise you, I'll always be here when you need me." His voice was as quiet as a sigh, but Cooper seemed almost to understand as he gave his father one of his rare smiles. Nick swallowed hard, walked to where Jacob lay in his crib watching them and whispered, "I love you guys. Both of you. And I'm going to find a way to make this work.

When Jake kicked his little legs and swung his arms, it was almost a celebration. At least, that's what Nick told himself.

That night Jenna pulled on her nightshirt and made one last check on the twins before going to bed herself, as was her habit. Only, this time when she stepped into the room lit only by a bunny nightlight, she found Nick already there.

He wasn't wearing a shirt. Just a pair of jeans that lay low on his hips and clung to his legs like a lover's hands. He turned when she stepped into the room, and she felt the power of his gaze slam into her. In the dim light, even his pale eyes were shadowed, dark, but she didn't need to see those eyes to feel the power in them. Her skin started humming, her blood sizzling, but she made herself put one foot in front of the other, walking past Nick first to Cooper's crib, then Jacob's, smoothing each of the boys' hair, laying a gentle hand on their tummies as they slept.

And through it all, she felt Nick's gaze on her as surely as she would have a touch. Her breath came in shallow gasps and her stomach did a quick enough spin that she felt nearly dizzy. What was he doing in here? Why was he watching her as he was? What was he thinking?

Her hands were shaking as she turned to leave the

nursery with quiet steps. She got as far as the hallway when Nick's hand came down on her arm.

"Wait." His voice was hard and low, demanding.

She looked up at him, and here in the dark, where even the pale light from the plugged-in plastic bunny couldn't reach, Nick was no more than a tall, imposing figure moving in close to her.

"Nick—" Could he hear her heartbeat? Could he sense the fires he kindled inside her? Could he feel the heat pouring off her body in thick waves? "What are you doing?"

Heaven help her, she knew what he was doing. And more, she was glad of it. Just standing with him in the dark filled her with a sense of expectation that had her breath catching in her lungs.

"Don't talk," he whispered, moving in even closer, until their bodies were pressed together, until he'd edged her back, up against the wall. "Don't think." He lifted both hands and covered her breasts.

She sucked in air and let her head thunk back against the wall. Even through the thin cotton fabric of her nightgown, she felt the thrill of anticipation washing through her. His hands were hot and hard and strong. His thumbs moved across the tips of her nipples and the scrape of the fabric over her sensitive skin was another kind of sweet agony.

"Yes, Nick," she whispered, licking dry lips and huffing in breaths as if she'd just finished running a marathon. "No thinking. Only feeling. I want—"

"Me, too," he said, cutting her off so fast, she knew

instinctively that he was feeling the immediacy of the moment. "Have for days. Can't wait another minute. I need to be in you, Jenna. To feel your heat around me." He dropped his head to the curve of her neck and swept his tongue across the pulse point at the base of her throat.

She jerked in his arms, then lifted her hands until she could cup the back of his head and hold him there. While her fingers threaded through his thick, dark hair, he dropped one hand down the front of her body, skimming her curves, lifting the hem of her nightshirt. Then he was touching her bare skin and she arched into him as he slid his magical fingers beneath the elastic band of her panties.

He touched her core, slid his fingers into her heat and instantly, she exploded, rocking her hips with the force of an orgasm that crashed down on her with a splintering fury. Whimpering his name, she clung to him with a desperate grip until the last of the tremors slid through her. Then she was limp against him until he picked her up and walked to her bedroom.

Holding on to him, Jenna smoothed her hands over his skin, his broad back, his sculpted chest, and when he sucked in a gulp of air, she smiled in the dark, pleased to know she affected him as deeply as he did her.

In moments she was on her bed, staring up at him as he tore his jeans off and came to her. In the next instant he'd pulled her nightshirt up and off, and slid her white lace panties down the length of her legs and tossed them onto the floor.

Since the second he'd walked, unannounced, into her home, Jenna had wanted this. She'd lain awake at night hungering for him, and now that he was here, she had no intention of denying either of them. Though, for all she knew, this was his way of saying goodbye. He might be getting ready to leave, to go back to his world.

And if that was the case, then she wanted this one last night with him. Wanted to feel him over and around her. Wanted to look up into those pale eyes and know that at least for this moment, she was the most important thing in the world to him.

Tomorrow could take care of itself.

He moved in between her legs and stroked her now all-too-sensitive center. She moaned softly, spread her legs farther and rocked her hips in silent invitation. All she wanted was to feel the hard, strong slide of his body into hers. To hold him within her.

Then he was there, plunging deep, stealing her breath with the hard thrusts of his body. He laid claim to her in the most ancient and intimate way. And Jenna gave him everything she had. Her hands stroked up and down his spine. Her short nails clawed at his skin. Her legs wrapped themselves around his hips and urged him deeper, higher.

When he bent his head to kiss her, she parted her lips and met his tongue with her own in a tangle of need and want that was so beyond passion, beyond desire, that she felt the incredible sense that *this* is where she'd always been meant to be.

He tore his mouth from hers, looked down into her eyes and said on a groan, "Jenna...I need you."

"You have me," she told him and then arched her spine as a soul-shattering climax hit them both hard. Holding him tight, Jenna called out his name as wave after wave of sensation crashed, receded and slammed down onto them again and again. She felt his release as well as her own. She held him as his body trembled and shook with a power that was mind numbing.

It seemed the pleasure would never end.

It seemed they were destined to be joined together for the rest of time.

But finally, inevitably, the tantalizing pressure and delight faded and they lay together in a silence so profound, neither of them knew how to end it.

Nick was gone when she woke up.

Not gone gone. His duffle bag was still in one corner of the living room, so he hadn't gone back to the ship. He was just nowhere to be found in the house. That shouldn't have surprised her. After all, he'd avoided her the morning after their night together on board ship, as well. But somehow, disappointment welled inside her, and she wondered if he was deliberately distancing himself from her. To make the inevitable leaving easier.

With the sting of unshed tears filling her eyes, she slipped into her normal routine of taking care of the boys, and tried not to remember how it had felt to have Nick there, sharing all of this with her.

Once the twins were fed and dressed, Jenna decided to get out of the house herself. Damned if she'd sit around the house moping, waiting for Nick to return so that he could break her heart by telling her he was leaving. She had a life of her own and she was determined to live it.

Buckling the boys into their car seats, she then grabbed up a stuffed diaper bag and her purse and fired up the engine on her car.

"Don't you worry, guys," she said, looking into the rearview mirror at the mirrors she had positioned in front of their car seats so that she could see their faces, "we're going to be fine. Daddy has to go away, but Mommy's here. And I'm never going to leave you."

Those blasted tears burned her eyes again and she blinked frantically to clear them away. She wasn't going to cry. She'd had an incredible night with the man she loved and she wasn't going to regret it. Whatever happened, happened.

When her cell phone rang, she assumed it was Maxie until she glanced at the screen and didn't recognize the number. "Hello?"

"Jenna."

"Nick," she said, and tried not to sigh at the sound of his deep, dark voice murmuring in her ear.

"You at home?"

"Actually," she said, lifting her chin as if that could help her keep her voice light and carefree, "I'm in the car. I'm taking the boys to the mall and—"

"Perfect," he said quickly. "Have you got a pen?"

"Yes, I have a pen, but what is this—"

"Write this down."

Both of her eyebrows lifted at the order. But she reached into her purse for a pen and a memo pad she always carried. Behind her Jacob was starting to fuss, and pretty soon, she knew, Cooper would be joining in. "Nick," she asked, pen poised, "what's this about?"

"Just…I want to show you something and I need you and the boys to come here."

"Here where?"

"Here in San Pedro."

She nearly groaned. "San Pedro?"

"Jenna, just do this for me, okay?" He paused, then added, "Please."

Surprise flickered through her. She couldn't remember Nick *ever* saying please before. So when he gave her directions, she dutifully wrote them down. When he was finished, she frowned and said, "Okay, we'll come. Should be there in about a half hour."

"I'll be waiting."

He hung up before she could ask any more questions, and Jenna scowled at her cell phone before she set it down on the seat beside her. "Well, guys, we're off to meet your father." Cooper cooed. "No, I don't know what this is about, either," she told her son. "But knowing your daddy, it could be anything."

It turned out to be a house.

Cape Cod style, it looked distinctly out of place in Southern California, but it was the most beautiful house Jenna had ever seen. It was huge, and she was willing to bet that five of her cottages would have fit comfortably inside. But for all its size, it looked like a family home. There was a wide front lawn, and when she stepped out of the car in the driveway, she heard the sound of the ocean and knew the big house must be right on the sea.

"What's going on here?" she wondered aloud. But then Jacob's short, sharp cry caught her attention and she turned to get her sons out of their seats.

"Jenna!"

She looked up and watched as Nick ran down the front lawn to her. He looked excited, his pale eyes shining, his mouth turned into a grin so wide, his dimple dug deeply into his left cheek. Naturally, Jenna felt an involuntary tug of emotion at first sight of him, and she wondered if it would always be that way.

God, she hoped not.

"Let me help with the boys," he said after giving her a quick, hard, unexpected kiss that left her reeling a little.

"Um, sure." She watched as he rounded the back of her car, opened the other back door and began undoing the straps on Cooper's car seat. "Nick, what's going on? Where are we? Whose house is this?"

He shot her another breath-stealing grin and scooped Cooper up into his arms. "I'll tell you everything as soon as we get inside."

"Inside?" Finished with Jacob's seat straps, she picked him up, cuddled him close and closed the car door with a loud smack of sound.

"Yep," Nick said. "Inside. Go on ahead. I'll get the diaper bag and your purse."

She took a step, stopped and looked at him. Dappled shade from the massive oak tree in the front yard fell across his features. He was wearing a tight black T-shirt and those faded jeans he'd been wearing the night before when they— *Okay, don't go there*, she told herself. "I can't just go inside. I don't know who lives here and—"

"Fine," he said, coming around the hood of the car, her purse under his arm and the diaper bag slung over that shoulder, while he jiggled Cooper on the other. "We'll go together. All of us. Better that way, anyway."

"What are you talking about?"

"You'll see." He started for the house and she had little choice but to follow.

The brick walkway from the drive to the front door was lined with primroses in vibrant, primary shades of color. More flowerbeds followed the line of the house, with roses and tall spires of pastel-colored stocks scenting the air with a heady perfume.

Jenna kept expecting the owner of the house to come to the front door to welcome them, but no one did. And when she crossed the threshold, she understood why.

The house was empty.

Their footsteps echoed in the cavernous rooms as Nick led her through the living room, past a wide staircase, down a hall and then through the kitchen. Her head turned from side to side, taking it all in, delighting in the space, the lines of the house. Whoever had designed it had known what they were doing. The walls were the color of rich, heavy cream, and dark wood framed doorways and windows. The floors were pale oak and polished to a high shine. The rooms bled one into the other in a flow that cried out for a family's presence.

This house was made for the sound of children's laughter. As Jenna followed Nick through room after room, she felt that there was a sense of ease in the house. As if the building itself were taking a deep breath and relishing the feel of people within its walls again.

"Nick…" The kitchen was amazing, but she hardly had time to glance at it as he led her straight through the big room and out the back door.

"Come on, I want you to see this," he said, stepping back so that she could move onto the stone patio in front of him.

A cold ocean wind slapped at her, and Jenna realized she'd been right, the house did sit on a knoll above the sea. The stone patio gave way to a rolling lawn edged with trees and flowers that looked as she imagined an English cottage garden would. Beyond the lawn was a low-lying fence with a gate that led to steps that would take the lucky people who lived here right down to the beach.

As Jenna held Jacob close, she did a slow turn, taking it all in, feeling overwhelmed with the beauty of the place as she finally circled back to look out at the sea, glittering with golden sunlight.

Shaking her head, she glanced at Nick. "I don't understand, Nick. What's going on? Why are we here?"

"Do you like it?" he asked, letting his gaze shift around the yard as he dropped the diaper bag and her purse to the patio. "The house, I mean," he said, hitching Cooper a little higher on his chest. "Do you like it?"

She laughed, uncertainty jangling her nerves. "What's not to like?"

"Good. That's good," he said, coming to her side. "Because I bought it."

"You—*what?*"

Nick nearly laughed at the stunned expression on her face. God, this had been worth all of the secretive phone calls to real estate agents he'd been making. Worth getting up and leaving her that morning so that he could finalize the deal with the house's former owners.

This was going to work.

It had to work.

"Why would you do that?"

"For us," he said, and had the pleasure of watching her features go completely slack as she staggered unsteadily for a second.

"*Us?*"

"Yes, Jenna. Us." He reached out, cupped her cheek in his palm and was only mildly disappointed when she stepped back and away from him. He would convince her. He *had* to convince her. "I found a solution to our situation," he said, locking his gaze with hers, wanting her to see everything he was thinking, feeling, written in his eyes.

"Our situation?" She blinked, shook her head as if to clear away cobwebs and then stared at him again.

The wind was cold, but the sun was warm. Shade from the trees didn't reach the patio, and the sunlight dancing in her hair made him want to grab her and hold her close. But first they had to settle this. Once and for all.

"The boys," he said, starting out slowly, as he'd planned. "We both love them. We both want them. So it occurred to me that the solution was for us to get married. Then we both have them."

She took another step back, and, irritated that she hadn't jumped on his plan wholeheartedly, Nick talked faster. "It's not like we don't get along. And the sex is great. You have to admit there's real chemistry between us, Jenna. It would work. You know it would."

"No," she shook her head again and when Jacob picked up on her tension and began to cry, Nick moved in closer to her.

He talked even faster, hurrying to change her mind. Make her see what their future could be. "Don't say no till you think about it, Jenna. When you do, you'll see that I'm right. This is perfect. For all of us."

"No, Nick," she said, soothing Jacob even as she smiled sadly up at him. "It's not perfect. I know you love your sons, I do. And I'm glad of that. They'll need you as much as you need them. But you don't love *me*."

"Jenna…"

"No." She laughed shortly, looked around the back-yard, at the sea, and then finally she turned her gaze on Nick again. "It doesn't matter if we get along, or if the sex and chemistry between us is great. I can't marry a man who doesn't love me."

Damn it. She was shutting him down, and he couldn't even find it in himself to blame her. Panic warred with desperation inside him and it was a feeling Nick wasn't used to. He was *never* the guy scrambling to make things work. People cowtowed to *him*. It didn't go the other way.

Yet here he stood, in front of this one woman, and knew deep down inside him that the only shot he'd have with her was if he played his last card.

"Oh, for—" Nick reached out with his free arm, snaked it around her shoulders and dragged her in close to him. So close that their bodies and the bodies of their sons all seemed to be melded together into a unit. "Fine. We'll do it the hard way, then. Damn it Jenna, I *do* love you."

"What?" Her eyes held a world of confusion and pain and something that looked an awful lot like hope.

She hadn't even looked that surprised when he'd shown up at her house a few days ago. That gave him hope. If he could keep her off balance, he could still win this. And suddenly Nick knew that he'd never wanted to win more; that nothing in his life had been this important. This huge. He had to say the right things now. Force her to listen. To really hear him. And to take a chance.

Staring down into her eyes, he took a breath, and then took the plunge. The leap that he'd never thought to make. "Of course I love you. What am I, an idiot?" He stopped, paused, and said, "Don't answer that."

"Nick, you don't have to—"

"Yeah, I do," he said quickly, feeling his moment sliding by. He hadn't wanted to have to admit to how he felt. He'd thought for sure that she'd go for the marriage-for-the-sake-of-the-boys thing and then he could have had all he wanted without mortgaging his soul. But maybe this was how it was supposed to work. Maybe you couldn't *get* love until you were willing to *give* it.

"Look, I'm not proud of this, but I've been trying to hide from what I feel for you since that first night we met more than a year ago." His gaze moved over her face and his voice dropped to a low rush of words that he hoped to hell convinced her that what he was saying was true. "I took one look at you and fell. Never meant to. Didn't want to. But I didn't have a choice. You were there, in the moonlight and it was as if I'd been waiting for you my whole damn life."

"But you—"

"Yeah," he said, knowing what she was going to say. "I pulled away. I let you go. Hell, I told myself I *wanted* you to go. But that was a lie." Laughing harshly, he said, "All this time, I've been calling you a liar, when the truth is, I'm the liar here. I lied to you. I lied to myself. Because I didn't want to let myself be vulnerable to you."

"Nick—" She swallowed hard and a single tear rolled down her cheek. He caught it with the pad of his thumb.

"It would have been much easier on me," he admitted, "if you'd accepted that half-assed, marriage-of-convenience proposal. Then I wouldn't have had to acknowledge what I feel for you. Wouldn't have to take the chance that you'll throw this back in my face."

"I wouldn't do that—"

"Wouldn't blame you if you did," he told her. "But since you didn't go along with my original plan, then I have to tell you everything. I love you, Jenna. Madly. Completely. Desperately."

Fresh tears welled, making her eyes shine, and everything in him began to melt. What power she had over him. Over his heart. And yet he didn't care anymore about protecting himself.

All that mattered was her.

"You walk into a room and everything else fades away," he said softly. "You gave me my sons. You gave me a glimpse into a world that I want to be a part of."

Another tear joined the first and then another and another. In her arms, Jacob hiccupped, screwed up his little face and started to cry in earnest. Quickly, Nick took the boy from her and cradled him in his free arm. Looking down at his boys, then to her, he said, "Just so you know, I'm not prepared to lose, here. Nick Falco doesn't quit when he wants something as badly as I want you. I won't let you go. Not any of you."

He glanced behind him at the sprawling house, then shifted his gaze back to her again as he outlined his master plan. "We'll live here. You can do your gift baskets in the house instead of the garage. There's a great room upstairs that looks over the ocean. Lots of space. Lots of direct light. It'd be perfect for you and all of your supplies."

She opened her mouth to speak, but Nick kept going before she could.

"I figure until the boys are in school, we can live half the year here, half on board ship. It'll be good for 'em. And if they like the dog I bought them, we'll take her along on the ship, too."

"You bought a d—"

"Golden retriever puppy," Nick said. "She's little now, but she'll grow."

"I can't believe—"

The words kept coming, tumbling one after the other from his mouth as he fought to convince her, battled to show her how their lives could be if she'd only take a chance on him.

"Once they're in school, we can cruise during the summers. I can run the line from here and I have Teresa. I'll promote her," he said fiercely. "She can do the on-board stuff and stay in touch via fax."

"But Nick—"

"And I want more kids," he said, and had the pleasure of seeing her mouth snap shut. "I want to be there from the beginning. I want to see our child growing within you. I want to be in the delivery room to watch him— or her—take that first breath. I want in on all of it, Jenna. I want to be with you. With them," he said, glancing at the twins he held cradled against him.

The boys were starting to squirm and he knew how they felt. Nick's world was balanced on a razor's edge, and he figured that he had only one more thing to say. "I'm not going to let you say no, Jenna. We belong together, you and me. I know you love me. And damn it, I love you, too. If you don't believe me, I'll find a way to convince you. But you're not getting away from me. Not again. I won't be without you, Jenna. I can't do it. I won't go back to that empty life."

The only sound then was the snuffling noises the twins were making and the roar of the sea rushing into the cliffs behind them. Nick waited what felt like a lifetime as he watched her eyes.

Then finally she smiled, moved in close to him and wrapped both arms around him and their sons. "You really are an idiot if you think I'd ever let you get away from me again."

Nick laughed, loud and long, and felt a thousand pounds of dread and worry slide from his shoulders. "You'll marry me."

"I will."

"And have more babies."

"Yes." She smiled up at him, and her eyes shone with a happiness so rich, so full, it stole Nick's breath. "A dozen if you want."

"And sail the world with me," he said, dipping his head to claim a kiss.

"Always," she said, still smiling, still shining with an inner light that warmed Nick through. "I love you, Nick. I always have. We'll be happy here, in this wonderful house."

"We will," he assured her, stealing another kiss.

"But you're going to be housetraining that puppy," she teased.

"For you, my love," Nick whispered, feeling his heart become whole for the first time in his life, *"anything."*

* * * * *

Don't miss Maureen Child's next release,
AN OFFICER AND A MILLIONAIRE,
on sale January 2009 from Silhouette Desire.

Turn the page for a sneak preview of
AFTERSHOCK, *a new anthology*
featuring New York Times *bestselling author*
Sharon Sala.

Available October 2008.

n●cturne™

Dramatic and sensual tales of paranormal romance.

Chapter 1

October
New York City

Nicole Masters was sitting cross-legged on her sofa while a cold autumn rain peppered the windows of her fourth-floor apartment. She was poking at the ice cream in her bowl and trying not to be in a mood.

Six weeks ago, a simple trip to her neighborhood pharmacy had turned into a nightmare. She'd walked into the middle of a robbery. She never even saw the man who shot her in the head and left her for dead. She'd survived, but some of her senses had not. She was dealing with short-term memory loss and a tendency to stagger.

Even though she'd been told the problems were most likely temporary, she waged a daily battle with depression.

Her parents had been killed in a car wreck when she was twenty-one. And except for a few friends—and most recently her boyfriend, Dominic Tucci, who lived in the apartment right above hers, she was alone. Her doctor kept reminding her that she should be grateful to be alive, and on one level she knew he was right. But he wasn't living in her shoes.

If she'd been anywhere else but at that pharmacy when the robbery happened, she wouldn't have died twice on the way to the hospital. Instead of being grateful that she'd survived, she couldn't stop thinking of what she'd lost.

But that wasn't the end of her troubles. On top of everything else, something strange was happening inside her head. She'd begun to hear odd things: sounds, not voices—at least, she didn't think it was voices. It was more like the distant noise of rapids—a rush of wind and water inside her head that, when it came, blocked out everything around her. It didn't happen often, but when it did, it was frightening, and it was driving her crazy.

The blank moments, which is what she called them, even had a rhythm. First there came that sound, then a cold sweat, then panic with no reason. Part of her feared it was the beginning of an emotional breakdown. And part of her feared it wasn't—that it was going to turn out to be a permanent souvenir of her resurrection.

Frustrated with herself and the situation as it stood, she upped the sound on the TV remote. But instead of *Wheel of Fortune,* an announcer broke in with a special bulletin.

"This just in. Police are on the scene of a kidnapping that occurred only hours ago at The Dakota. Molly Dane, the six-year-old daughter of one of Hollywood's blockbuster stars, Lyla Dane, was taken by force from the family apartment. At this time they have yet to receive a ransom demand. The housekeeper was seriously injured during the abduction, and is, at the present time, in surgery. Police are hoping to be able to talk to her once she regains consciousness. In the meantime, we are going now to a press conference with Lyla Dane."

Horrified, Nicole stilled as the cameras went live to where the actress was speaking before a bank of microphones. The shock and terror in Lyla Dane's voice were physically painful to watch. But even though Nicole kept upping the volume, the sound continued to fade.

Just when she was beginning to think something was wrong with her set, the broadcast suddenly switched from the Dane press conference to what appeared to be footage of the kidnapping, beginning with footage from inside the apartment.

When the front door suddenly flew back against the wall and four men rushed in, Nicole gasped. Horrified, she quickly realized that this must have been caught on a security camera inside the Dane apartment.

As Nicole continued to watch, a small Asian woman, who she guessed was the maid, rushed forward in an effort to keep them out. When one of the men hit her in the face with his gun, Nicole moaned. The violence was too reminiscent of what she'd lived through. Sick to her stomach, she fisted her hands against her belly, wishing it was over, but unable to tear her gaze away.

When the maid dropped to the carpet, the same man followed with a vicious kick to the little woman's mid-section that lifted her off the floor.

"Oh, my God," Nicole said. When blood began to pool beneath the maid's head, she started to cry.

As the tape played on, the four men split up in different directions. The camera caught one running down a long marble hallway, then disappearing into a room. Moments later he reappeared, carrying a little girl, who Nicole assumed was Molly Dane. The child was wearing a pair of red pants and a white turtleneck sweater, and her hair was partially blocking her abductor's face as he carried her down the hall. She was kicking and screaming in his arms, and when he slapped her, it elicited an agonized scream that brought the other three running. Nicole watched in horror as one of them ran up and put his hand over Molly's face. Seconds later, she went limp.

One moment they were in the foyer, then they were gone.

Nicole jumped to her feet, then staggered drunkenly. The bowl of ice cream she'd absentmindedly placed in her lap shattered at her feet, splattering glass and melting ice cream everywhere.

The picture on the screen abruptly switched from the kidnapping to what Nicole assumed was a rerun of Lyla Dane's plea for her daughter's safe return, but she was numb.

Before she could think what to do next, the doorbell rang. Startled by the unexpected sound, she shakily swiped at the tears and took a step forward. She didn't feel the glass shards piercing her feet until she took the second step. At that point, sharp pains shot through her foot. She gasped, then looked down in confusion. Her legs looked as if she'd been running through mud, and she was standing in broken glass and ice cream, while a thin ribbon of blood seeped out from beneath her toes.

"Oh, no," Nicole mumbled, then stifled a second moan of pain.

The doorbell rang again. She shivered, then clutched her head in confusion.

"Just a minute!" she yelled, then tried to sidestep the rest of the debris as she hobbled to the door.

When she looked through the peephole in the door, she didn't know whether to be relieved or regretful.

It was Dominic, and as usual, she was a mess.

Nicole smiled a little self-consciously as she opened the door to let him in. "I just don't know what's happening to me. I think I'm losing my mind."

"Hey, don't talk about my woman like that."

Nicole rode the surge of delight his words brought. "So I'm still your woman?"

Dominic lowered his head.
Their lips met.
The kiss proceeded.
Slowly.
Thoroughly.

*****

Be sure to look for the
AFTERSHOCK *anthology next month,*
as well as other exciting paranormal stories
from Silhouette Nocturne.
Available in October wherever books are sold.

nocturne™

NEW YORK TIMES BESTSELLING AUTHOR

SHARON SALA

JANIS REAMES HUDSON
DEBRA COWAN

—

AFTERSHOCK

Three women are brought to the brink of death...
only to discover the aftershock of their trauma has
left them with unexpected and unwelcome gifts of
paranormal powers. Now each woman must learn to
accept her newfound abilities while fighting for life,
love and second chances....

Available October wherever books are sold.

www.eHarlequin.com
www.paranormalromanceblog.wordpress.com   SN61796

Harlequin® Historical
Historical Romantic Adventure!

HALLOWE'EN HUSBANDS

With three fantastic stories by

Lisa Plumley
Denise Lynn
Christine Merrill

Don't miss these unforgettable stories about three women who experience the mysterious happenings of Allhallows Eve and come to discover that finding true love on this eerie day is not so scary after all.

Look for
HALLOWE'EN HUSBANDS

Available October
wherever books are sold.

Inside ROMANCE

Stay up-to-date on all your romance reading news!

The Inside Romance newsletter is a FREE quarterly newsletter highlighting our upcoming series releases and promotions!

Click on the <u>Inside Romance</u> link on the front page of **www.eHarlequin.com** or e-mail us at insideromance@harlequin.ca to sign up to receive your FREE newsletter today!

You can also subscribe by writing us at: HARLEQUIN BOOKS
Attention: Customer Service Department
P.O. Box 9057, Buffalo, NY 14269-9057

Please allow 4-6 weeks for delivery of the first issue by mail.

IRNBPA108

REQUEST YOUR FREE BOOKS!

2 FREE NOVELS PLUS 2 FREE GIFTS!

Passionate, Powerful, Provocative!

YES! Please send me 2 FREE Silhouette Desire® novels and my 2 FREE gifts (gifts are worth about $10). After receiving them, if I don't wish to receive any more books, I can return the shipping statement marked "cancel". If I don't cancel, I will receive 6 brand-new novels every month and be billed just $4.05 per book in the U.S. or $4.74 per book in Canada, plus 25¢ shipping and handling per book and applicable taxes, if any*. That's a savings of almost 15% off the cover price! I understand that accepting the 2 free books and gifts places me under no obligation to buy anything. I can always return a shipment and cancel at any time. Even if I never buy another book, the two free books and gifts are mine to keep forever. 225 SDN ERVX 326 SDN ERVM

Name	(PLEASE PRINT)
Address	Apt. #
City	State/Prov. Zip/Postal Code

Signature (if under 18, a parent or guardian must sign)

Mail to the Silhouette Reader Service:
IN U.S.A.: P.O. Box 1867, Buffalo, NY 14240-1867
IN CANADA: P.O. Box 609, Fort Erie, Ontario L2A 5X3

Not valid to current subscribers of Silhouette Desire books.

Want to try two free books from another line?
Call 1-800-873-8635 or visit www.morefreebooks.com.

* Terms and prices subject to change without notice. N.Y. residents add applicable sales tax. Canadian residents will be charged applicable provincial taxes and GST. Offer not valid in Quebec. This offer is limited to one order per household. All orders subject to approval. Credit or debit balances in a customer's account(s) may be offset by any other outstanding balance owed by or to the customer. Please allow 4 to 6 weeks for delivery. Offer available while quantities last.

Your Privacy: Silhouette Books is committed to protecting your privacy. Our Privacy Policy is available online at www.eHarlequin.com or upon request from the Reader Service. From time to time we make our lists of customers available to reputable third parties who may have a product or service of interest to you. If you would prefer we not share your name and address, please check here. ☐

SDES08R

SPECIAL EDITION™

BRAVO FAMILY TIES

Tanner Bravo and Crystal Cerise had it bad
for each other, though they couldn't be more
different. Tanner was the type to settle down;
free-spirited Crystal wouldn't hear of it.
Now that Crystal was pregnant, would
Tanner have his way after all?

Look for

HAVING
TANNER BRAVO'S
BABY

by *USA TODAY* bestselling author
CHRISTINE RIMMER

Available in October wherever books are sold.

Visit Silhouette Books at www.eHarlequin.com   SSE24927

Silhouette°
nocturne™ BITES

Introducing Nocturne Bites eBooks...
dark, sexy and not quite human...

If you are looking for a short but sensual
taste of the paranormal, satisfy your craving
with Nocturne Bites eBooks,
available online at

www.nocturnebites.com

Indulge in original short stories by
these fabulous Nocturne authors:

DREAMCATCHER BY ANNA LEONARD
Available September

MAHINA'S STORM BY VIVI ANNA
Available October

DEADLY TOUCH BY BONNIE ANNE VANAK
Available November

HELLBOUND BY LORI DEVOTI
Available December

A dark, sexy indulgence, these short
paranormal romances are a feast for the
romantic soul...download a Bite today!

SNBITE08

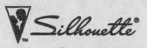

Silhouette®

Romantic
SUSPENSE

**Sparked by Danger,
Fueled by Passion.**

USA TODAY bestselling author

Merline Lovelace

Undercover Wife

CODENAME:
DANGER

Secret agent Mike Callahan, code name Hawkeye,
objects when he's paired with sophisticated
Gillian Ridgeway on a dangerous spy mission
to Hong Kong. Gillian has secretly been in love
with him for years, but Hawk is an overprotective
man with a wounded past that threatens to
resurface. Now the two must put their lives—
and hearts—at risk for each other.

Available October wherever books are sold.

COMING NEXT MONTH

#1897 MARRIAGE, MANHATTAN STYLE—Barbara Dunlop
Park Avenue Scandals
Secrets, blackmail and infertility had their marriage on the rocks.
Will an unexpected opportunity at parenthood give them a second
chance?

#1898 THE MONEY MAN'S SEDUCTION—Leslie LaFoy
Gifts from a Billionaire
Suspicious of her true motives, he vows to keep her close—but as
close as in his bed?

#1899 DANTE'S CONTRACT MARRIAGE—Day Leclaire
The Dante Legacy
Forced to marry to protect an infamous diamond, they never
counted on being struck by The Dante Inferno. Suddenly their
convenient marriage is full of *in*convenient passion.

#1900 AN AFFAIR WITH THE PRINCESS—Michelle Celmer
Royal Seductions
He'd had an affair with the princess, once upon a time. But why
had he returned? Remembrance...or revenge?

#1901 MISTAKEN MISTRESS—Tessa Radley
The Saxon Brides
Could this woman he feels such a reckless passion for really be
his late brother's mistress? Or are there other secrets she's hiding?

#1902 BABY BENEFITS—Emily McKay
Billionaires and Babies
Her boss had a baby—and he needed her help. How could she
possibly deny him...how could she ever resist him?

SDCNM0908